Arizona Pay-Off

When Tex Scarron, six feet of whipcord and steel, rode home to the Bar X in Arizona, he found Parson Dean and his gang working a lucrative 'protection' racket. Any rancher who failed to pay up had his cattle rustled, his homestead burnt about his ears and his cowhands shot in the back.

Tex's earlier experience fighting hoodlums came in handy, and the gunplay was fast and furious before he rid the territory of the Parson, solved the mystery that lay behind the racket, and incidentally found happiness with the mysterious outlaw girl whose trail had so often crossed his own.

Arizona Pay-Off

Duke Patterson

ROBERT HALE · LONDON

First published 1954
This edition published in Great Britain 2009

ISBN 978-0-7090-8780-9

Robert Hale Limited
Clerkenwell House
Clerkenwell Green
London EC1R 0HT

www.halebooks.com

Typeset by
Derek Doyle & Associates, Shaw Heath
Printed and bound in Great Britain by
CPI Antony Rowe, Chippenham and Eastbourne

CHAPTER 1

'Watch it, pal, if you're aimin' to take the Black Hills trail ridin' alone. Maybe bein' a stranger you ain't heard o' the Kid, but I guess everyone else in Arizona has. There's been word he was sighted hangin' around here . . . watch it, he's mighty dangerous.'

Tex Scarron, six feet of whipcord and steel, at thirty experienced and in his prime, was thinking about this warning as later he rode solitary along the Black Hills trail. The bartender back at Indian Creek, the settlement now left behind, hadn't been faking. He believed that the Kid had been seen in the district – and maybe he was right at that – and he'd got ants in his pants as a result.

Tex grunted at his own thoughts as he rode the trail towards the hills looming ahead. The moon was up, shedding a silvery radiance over the trail itself, thick with the alkali dust after a hot day, over the broken, waste ground lying on either side, over the hills, outcrops of the Mexican Sierra Madre range which broke across the border between Mexico and Arizona. Tex didn't need telling that here was ideal country for a hold-up, for the operations of bandits. The terrain itself was highly suitable, broken, deserted; furthermore this corner of the great state of Arizona was isolated, cut off from civilization, inhabited only by ranchers who had the reputation of keeping themselves to themselves and running their own affairs.

Tex was aiming for the township of Grant's River, on the other side of the Black Hills. It was true that he was a stranger to Arizona, in that he hadn't set foot in the state for twenty years, but that didn't mean he hadn't heard of the notorious Kid, bandit and outlaw, who operated almost exclusively in Arizona. The Kid's name was known elsewhere in the Union; and Tex had been around.

He'd heard of the Kid, knew that the guy had been at work for a good few years, evading all attempts to get him. He'd been wise to select Arizona, for the Governor, who had recently handed in his checks, hadn't been exactly efficient. Parts of the state had sunk back into lawlessness during his term of office.

All this Tex knew because he'd made it his business to find out, ever since the letter Sam Steel had sent him had caught up with him. What Sam had said in that letter had made it necessary for Tex to find out what he could about the Arizona set-up. Now a new Governor, of the name of York, had been appointed and they said he was a go-getter. Maybe in future the Kid wouldn't find it so easy to make a living hi-jacking and looting; and maybe certain guys in Grant's River would find it necessary to pull in their horns.

Tex wasn't worrying much about the Kid. Tex had mixed with all sorts and knew his stuff. His two Colts were lying loose in their holsters as he rode towards the hills, and there weren't many guys quicker on the draw than Scarron. He'd been in contact with bandits before, knew that the majority were jackals when it came to it. A guy who knew how to look after himself wasn't usually in much danger. It was true that the Kid had managed pretty well up to now, true that rumour had it that he always worked alone or with a single companion, not like most running in with a gang. Maybe this was true and the guy had more guts than most, but Tex wasn't worrying. He didn't reckon the Kid or anyone else would stop him getting to Grant's River tonight and then to the Bar X.

He dismissed the Kid from his mind and concentrated on the Bar X set-up, the Grant's River set-up, as laboriously outlined by Sam in his letter. Sam was a better hand with a six-shooter or a lariat than with the pen, but he'd managed to put down what he wanted. He'd appealed to Tex, reminding him of the old days of boyhood, when Tex had spent three years with his uncle at the Bar X. He hadn't appealed in vain, but Tex was sorry the letter had taken so long to catch up with him. In three months quite a lot could have happened at Grant's River. According to Sam things had been pretty bad when the letter was written. Old Dave, Tex's mother's brother, had folded up. By now maybe things were worse.

For the time being the fact that Arizona had a new Governor, who according to reports was out to clean-up the state, wasn't important. Tex was always willing to take on anything himself, do his own cleaning-up when necessary; but the mechanism of the law wasn't to be despised – when it was in working order. To bump off a crook was OK when there was nothing else for it, but the example of a public trial was often valuable. Maybe it would work out that this guy Sam called the Parson could be attended to by York . . . in the end. But first the set-up had to be investigated and the Parson proved guilty.

Tex's pony picked its own way along the narrow trail. Man and beast had ridden a long way during the day and both were tired, though at Indian Creek they had found refreshment and some rest. Tex could have stayed the night at the Creek, but that wasn't his way. When he was on a job he always wanted to get to it without delay. This job interested him more than any other he had taken on during the last ten years of free-lancing, looking for trouble; Dave Brand had been kind to him in the old days. Already enough time had been wasted.

Pony and rider moved on up the trail which since Indian Creek had been rising, making for the pass in the hills. The moon gave the area a quality which the scorching sun of summer could not, for the moon's art lay in concealment. Now the barren ground, here on this side of the Black Hills unsuitable for cattle grazing, was given a soft quality, the harsh lines of canyons and gaunt rocks made more gentle by the silver light. Nevertheless it was not inviting country. Good country for the Kid or any other bandit, certainly. There was money in the Grant's River area. Sure, money . . . that was what also brought Tex Scarron here.

After nearly an hour Tex reached a point within a quarter of a mile of the crest of the pass. Ahead of him lay the beginning of the defile through which the trail passed. Precipitous cliffs ran down sheer to the trail on either side, forming a gorge through which ran the trail.

Tex pulled up to check over his guns. If he were a bandit aiming to lay up along this trail, well used by ranchers, he'd choose the defile as the ambush site, and he remembered that near the crest of the pass was a cleft in the right-hand cliff, offering a handy escape route to the west. Tex was always careful.

He checked his Colts . . . and then, from behind him he heard the clatter of a pony's hoofs drawing near. He couldn't see who was coming for he was on the wrong side of a bend in the trail, but whoever it was either liked hurrying or needed to make speed. It was just about ten o'clock now, not very late but late enough for precautions to be taken along a trail like this.

Tex swung off his beast and made for cover. He found it within a few yards of the trail, a cluster of gigantic rocks, affording concealment for both him and his pony. He left the beast free for the pony was well trained. It stood quietly, not attempting to move. Tex himself crouched behind one of the rocks, his Colt in his hand, his eyes on the snaking trail leading back to Indian Creek.

The clatter of hoofs came on, not hesitating. Then round the bend swirled a rider, clearly to be seen in the moonlight. Rider and pony came round the bend and then the latter was pulled in sharply and skilfully. It reared up but remained under perfect control. The rider swung lightly from the saddle, eyes on the dusty trail.

Tex Scarron's jaw tightened, his brows drew together in sheer surprise. The rider who had come up solitary, mounted on a beast obviously fresh and mettlesome, who had controlled the animal with such skill, was a mere slip of a girl, standing maybe five foot five, no more; a slender girl, not at all bad looking, in fact pretty much the other way unless the moonlight was playing tricks. Tex stayed where he was for a few moments, too surprised to move.

He knew the West intimately, knew that girls such as this didn't usually ride about the place alone after dark. Ranchers in all the cow states were mighty careful about their wives and daughters, they had to be. No respectable girl would be out alone at this hour on a trail such as this, not if she could help it. This girl was respectable all right. Tex hadn't a doubt about that. It might be that some accident had happened, accounting for her riding along this trail; but somehow the impression Tex gained was that she was here deliberately, not the victim of circumstances but in control of them. He couldn't rightly have explained why he was so sure, but he was.

Then with further surprise he realized that she was trailing him.

She was casting round, eyes on the ground; she was picking up the tracks he had left in the white dust. Now she was standing gazing towards the huddle of rocks . . . and in her hand had appeared a gun.

Tex reckoned it was time he moved. He hadn't yet been flushed out of anywhere by a woman and he wasn't going to start now. He didn't trust women with firearms. He'd play this game his own way; and his curiosity was aroused. He wanted to know more about this girl.

He moved silently, with the uncanny stealth he had learned over the years. His pony remained standing motionless, out of sight – not that it mattered now if the beast was seen because already Tex was way off the line. For all his bulk, his six feet of height and two hundred pounds avoirdupois, he moved without a sound. The girl didn't hear him, didn't see him. He moved down the slope, and came to a point thirty yards from where he had originally crouched. He was still under cover.

He saw the girl move also, cautiously, gun still levelled. She moved carefully towards the huddle of rocks. Mighty soon now she'd sight the pony. Tex put up his own gun. He had scruples about even threatening a woman with a Colt. He could manage all right without the aid of the gun.

She passed out of sight behind the first boulder of the cluster and then Tex came to his feet. As lightly as a cat he moved up the slope again, came to the boulders once more and saw the girl standing by the pony only five yards away. She was peering this way and that – but not behind her, which was her mistake.

Tex stuck his hands in his gun-belt and moved into sight.

'Evenin', miss . . . lookin' for somethin'?'

At that she swung round, surprised but not at a loss, he noted. He also noted that her hair, escaping from under her wide-brimmed Stetson, was very dark, almost black, framing a small, oval face pale in the moonlight. Her eyes could be brown or dark blue, he estimated. He couldn't be sure about that yet.

She certainly wasn't at a loss. The little gun didn't waver, jerked up menacingly.

'Get your hands up,' she snapped.

Tex kept his hands in his belt. He laughed, but his eyes were wary and shrewd, fixed on the gun. As he spoke he moved forward, very slowly.

'I guess I got a rooted objection to takin' orders, especially from women,' he drawled. 'But come to that I don't reckon you're a woman . . . what's the reckonin', 'bout eighteen, maybe? I should say your Dad don't know you're out?'

Deliberately he made his voice taunting. He judged that being female, if not strictly speaking yet a woman, she wouldn't much like what he'd said or the way he'd said it. That ought to make her drop her guard a bit.

He was right, she was mad – and she dropped her guard.

'Don't you talk to me like that,' she said, her voice angry, though Tex reckoned that in other circumstances it could be melodious.

That was as far as she got, for Tex had taken the chance afforded by her attention moving from him and what he was doing to what he had said. He moved like lightning . . . reached her in a couple of strides and his hand had plucked the gun from her grasp before she rightly knew what was happening.

It was all over inside a couple of seconds; and Tex was slipping the gun into the pocket of his jeans.

'Guess we can talk more easily now,' he drawled. 'Dangerous things guns – when females start handlin' 'em.'

She still exhibited no fear, but there was anger showing in her eyes, blazing anger.

'Give me back that gun,' she ordered. 'I'll. . . .'

'Cut it out, miss, you'll do nothin'. What you reckon you are, Deadwood Dick?' He looked at her more closely, noting the slender column of her white throat rising from the open neck of her check shirt, the bud-sharp figure and the lines of a body which couldn't be much more than his first guess of her age. He saw, too, that her eyes were in fact blue. 'I like blue,' he continued abruptly, 'blue eyes, I mean.'

She bit her lip – it was a generous, red mouth. But before she could speak Tex had continued.

'Suppose you tell me what you were trailin' me for? I'm a stranger in these parts, leastways, I haven't been here for twenty years, not since I was a boy stayin' with my uncle at the Bar X. I reckon I ain't given you any cause to come after me with a gun.'

Her manner changed somewhat, he could sense it. She stared at him, at last spoke.

'The Bar X? You mean Dave Brand is your uncle?'

'Sure, I'm aimin' to pay him a visit . . . it's about time I did.' She could make what she liked of this last remark. 'Well, what about the trailin', Miss . . . what's the name? Mine's Scarron, Tex Scarron they call me.'

She didn't exactly relax but she grew less alert.

'All right, I'll take your word for it,' she said. 'I'm Linda Forbes, from the Lazy Y . . . my cousin owns it.' Then, as a thought obviously came to her, 'Who owned it in your day?'

'Ted Wyatt, they called him Dutch . . . satisfied?'

'Yes, Buck bought it off Wyatt. OK stranger, I guess you're telling the truth.' She held out her hand. 'How about my gun?'

He didn't make any move to give it back to her. She still hadn't answered the most important of the questions he had put to her.

'Why did you trail me?' he repeated.

'I saw you from way back . . . there's talk the Kid is around. I aimed to find out who was ridin' the trail, that's all. You left your tracks in the alkali.'

Tex grunted. So far so good; he was willing to believe the story, but it still seemed queer she was out alone after dark; queer, too, that she, a slip of a girl, had been willing to take such a risk and handle a gun so casually. Unless Arizona had changed a whole lot since Tex's day, ranchers didn't much care for their womenfolk using rods.

Apparently she read his thoughts with some accuracy.

'I can look after myself,' she stated, 'and maybe I can use a gun better than you can, Mister Scarron. You said just now maybe my Dad didn't know I was out. I've got no parents and Buck gave up tryin' to keep me in a long time ago.'

She spoke with the sing-song accent of the Arizona cow-country, but her voice, very clear and as Tex had guessed melodious when she wasn't angry, lent it a quality usually absent when ranchers talked. Tex watched her with interest. She was mighty sure of herself; and remembering how she had controlled her pony he thought maybe she could handle a gun.

'May I have it back please?' she asked again.

'Sure . . . sorry I took it, but I wasn't takin' risks.' He paused for a moment and then added, 'What I said just before I grapped it wasn't meant personal . . . I was aimin' to get your attention off what I was doin'.'

Her blue eyes were shrewd as she returned his gaze. Then for a moment a little smile touched her lips.

'OK. You pulled a fast one. I don't like bein' foxed, but. . . .'

'But this time you'll call it quits? I'm mighty glad about that. I guess we'd better be friends, seein' I'm going to stay at the Bar X for a bit. How about it, Linda? You're not too old to mind me usin' your first name?'

He towered over her, seven or maybe eight inches taller than she, a massive man but as she could see without an ounce of fat on him. His hair, showing in the moonlight, for he had taken off his Stetson, glinted with a dull red sheen. His face was strong and intelligent.

She dropped her eyes suddenly, involuntarily. And as she did so a faint flush showed on her cheeks. Tex Scarron was the first man who had ever brought colour to Linda's face.

'Of course I don't mind,' she said slowly.

'That's fine . . . I told you, folks call me Tex. I'm hoping we shall see somethin' of each other. Sam Steel wrote me about some o' the folks hereabouts, but he didn't say nothin' 'bout you. It's been a pleasant surprise.' He broke off for an instant and then continued. 'He told me there's a guy they call Parson Dean down at Grant's River . . . seems he owns the hotel and the gamblin' joint as well. Guess you know the Parson?'

He made his voice sound casual and, as he spoke, he handed her back her gun. His voice was casual, but he was watching her closely.

He could do with her reactions to the name of Parson Dean, seeing she was outside the Bar X set-up and, presumably, the Parson's field of operations. The reactions of an outsider were often valuable.

She didn't answer for a moment but took the gun and held it loosely. Then she spoke.

'Everyone knows the Parson,' she said. 'He's a good enough guy, I guess. Some folk are jealous of him, that's the way it usually goes, but he's brought a bit of law and order to the River . . . before he came there was trouble with bandits, but he's put a stop to that.'

Tex said nothing at all, but he was thinking pretty hard. What Linda Forbes had said didn't link up with the report Sam had sent through. Well, maybe the girl didn't know the real facts and had swallowed the tale that Parson Dean was doing the settlement and the ranchers a good turn with his mutual protection scheme.

Linda spoke again, switching the subject. Her grasp tightened on the butt of the gun.

'Maybe I'd better prove I can handle a rod,' she said.

She brought up the gun and the next instant it had cracked viciously. Two hundred yards away a straight wooden pole, stuck in the earth and left there, maybe by some rancher to mark a boundary, splintered as the bullet struck home.

It was first-class shooting, pretty nearly miraculous for a girl. Tex wouldn't have backed himself to hit a target only inches wide at such a range.

'Well, Tex, good enough?' asked the girl. 'You reckon I'm safe with a gun?'

She might have continued, but as the last words were spoken, from the far distance there came the crack of another shot. Almost it was like the echo of Linda's. Somebody else was shooting, maybe for target practice but maybe not.

Tex swung round, automatically his hand reaching for one of his Colts. As he did so another shot was heard . . . and then another.

Tex Scarron was remembering that the Kid was reported to be in the district. Tex grabbed for his pony, standing by. He wanted to know what was going on over the other side of the Black Hills pass.

CHAPTER 2

'You stay right where you are,' snapped Tex to the girl, as he swung into the saddle. 'Maybe there's trouble and you don't want to be mixed up in it.'

Linda didn't reply – for one thing she had no chance – for Tex continued swiftly, 'Or maybe you'd best get back to the Lazy Y pronto . . . you can make it without touching the pass?'

'Yes, there's another way, the route I used coming.'

'OK, get movin' then . . . I oughtn't to leave you, but I got to find out what's cookin'.'

The girl smiled briefly.

'I can look after myself, I don't need a nurse.'

Tex hesitated. He wasn't used to having girls around the place when he was moving into action. His first instinct had been to go straight into action; but then he'd realized that according to the rules he oughtn't to leave Linda to fend for herself. Certainly he wasn't taking her with him over the pass. He hesitated in spite of what she had said and in spite of the proof she had given that she could indeed look after herself; but then came yet another shot from over the pass. Something was cooking all right, and it could be that the Kid was operating.

Linda made up his mind for him. Without warning she gave his pony a cut across the rump with the switch she took from the top of her boot. The animal reared and then was away. The last Tex saw of the girl for some little time was as she ran to her own beast and mounted, swinging down the trail away from the pass.

It looked like that was that. She was away and it was doubtful if he could catch her even if he tried. He comforted himself with the memory of the way she had handled the gun. He pressed on up the sloping trail, entering the defile. He judged that the shots had come from the other side of the pass, which meant he ought to be able to negotiate the dangerous gorge safely and without interference. There might be an alternative route bypassing the defile but he didn't know and had no time to explore.

He got through the pass without incident, however, came to a point beyond the highest point from where he could see the flat country beyond, ranching country running down to Grant's River and past the settlement for many miles.

Tex halted for a few moments, ears strained, eyes peering. No more shots came, but he had not imagined those heard earlier.

He pushed on more cautiously, until he came within a hundred yards of a sharp bend in the trail ahead. The cliffs had now dropped back and on either side of the trail was broken foothill ground showing jagged outcrops huddled close, though between them was open ground. The area offered the possibility of cover and also of some manoeuvre, unlike the defile through which Tex had recently passed.

He dismounted, led his pony towards the bend and then left the beast while he himself proceeded on foot. Those taking part in the shooting might well have moved quite a way during the interval occupied by Tex in reaching his present position, but on the other hand no move might yet have been made. According to his judgment the shots had been fired mighty near to where he now was. He was taking no chances.

Clustered at the bend were rocks. He reached them and cautiously negotiated the bend well under cover. He got into position from where he could see the trail beyond the bend stretching straight, running slightly downhill. What he saw made him glad he'd taken precautions.

Three hundred yards down the trail two men stood with their hands up, their ponies tethered nearby. Two other men, mounted, had their guns out, covering the others. Tex Scarron's eyes narrowed as he saw in the moonlight that masks covered the features of the mounted guys and that one of them was dressed all in black, without a spot of colour to relieve it. It was well-known that the Kid favoured black.

His companion dismounted as Tex watched, swung lightly to the ground and with his gun still in one hand approached the prisoners. He began to frisk the first, whom Tex could see was a gigantic man, larger even than himself and he judged much heavier. The other was shorter by a good foot, as thin as a lath, with hunched shoulders and a lean face which under the moon showed pallid.

It looked like the Kid and his accomplice had only just got around to grabbing their victims, otherwise they'd have been frisked earlier. Some sort of a fight must have been put up. Tex reckoned he'd arrived on the scene at just about the right moment.

He backed away from the rocks. He had little doubt that the notorious Kid himself was at work. Both he and his companion had black kerchiefs tied so that only their eyes showed. Tex knew that even at close quarters it would be impossible to identify them – until the masks were ripped away. He aimed to make sure that before long the kerchiefs were taken off. The Kid was going to be unlucky tonight, he hoped.

There was no point in launching a frontal attack; caution would have to be used for a bit.

There was plenty of cover and Tex used it skilfully. He left his beast where it was, but took the precaution of tethering it. Then on foot still he moved away from the trail, cut across the neck of the sharp loop, sticking closely to the cover of outcrops and boulders and came within sight of the group on the trail once more. The Kid's companion, whose garments were more orthodox in that they weren't all black, was now at work robbing, going through the pockets of the giant, while the Kid himself, provided that Tex was right and it was the Kid, kept both victims covered, still in the saddle.

Tex used all the skill he had. He had chosen that side of the trail which lay behind the two bandits, whose backs were now to him. Evidently they had no suspicion what was afoot.

Eventually Tex came to a rock not more than fifty yards from the trail and from the group. Now he was sitting pretty. All he had to do was wing the bandits, first the Kid himself and then his companion. After that it would be easy. Fortunately the victims of the hold-up were not masking the bandits.

Tex brought up his Colt. He had all the time in the world to pull his fast one, didn't reckon he could miss at this range. He settled himself carefully, drew a bead on the Kid.

And then without warning there came a dramatic interruption. From behind Tex came the crack of a gun. A bullet flaked a chip from the rock behind which he had taken cover. It missed his head by a matter of inches only.

His reflexes were swift, experience stood him in good stead. Automatically, instinctively, he flung himself flat, twisted over and was under cover again, this time from the new menace which had materialized from behind him. As he twisted another shot was fired, but this time the bullet spurted dust from the ground some yards away.

Tex saw the flash of the enemy gun and fired instantly. What result there was he didn't know. He heard nothing, saw nothing. Whoever had attacked, almost certainly, he reckoned, another of the Kid's guys who must have watched the manoeuvres, was well under cover. The second shot had come from behind a line of outcrops some hundred yards in the rear.

From the trail itself there now came the sounds of commotion. Tex heaved himself round, was just in time to see the two bandits wrenching round their horses, the second having mounted. Tex fired twice, but missed, for now the Kid and his companion were moving and the moonlight was deceptive, not bright enough for accurate shooting against moving targets.

As Tex brought up his Colt again a third shot cracked out from behind him and he had to duck back under cover. As he ducked he glimpsed the bandits disappearing round the next bend in the trail.

He cursed himself bitterly. He had been so occupied in getting into position to attack that he hadn't even considered the possibility that the Kid had left somebody to guard his flanks and rear.

The victims of the hold-up were making for their ponies, but Tex didn't bother about them just yet. The Kid's accomplice was still somewhere around and Tex wanted him. There wasn't a chance of catching up with the Kid, but the guy who must have trailed Tex himself might be grabbed, given luck. Tex went after him.

He slid sideways, reached cover some yards from the first rock and had the satisfaction of hearing another shot fired from the outcrop. The third guy was still sitting up there, then, which was OK by Tex. He pin-pointed the flash of the gun and moved again.

Again there could be no frontal attack; he must get round to the flank and then behind the man laying for him. He went to it grimly.

With infinite caution but as fast as possible he moved, always under cover, to the flank, then made up the slope. He passed the line of the outcrops, came behind them. He glimpsed a movement fifty yards to his right, saw for a brief moment a shadowy figure but didn't use his gun for the next instant the shadow had gone to earth behind an outcrop.

Tex's lips drew back in a characteristic gesture. He wasn't going to slip up this time. He moved on along the outcrops. Loose stones and small rocks lay around but Tex didn't make a false step. At last he came to a spot from which he could see very plainly the hoodlum who had interfered so decisively in his own plans. He was only ten yards from the crouching figure.

For the second time in less than an hour Tex was startled, and for the same reason. It was no hoodlum taking cover behind the outcrop . . . it was the girl, Linda Forbes.

The shock caused him to relax his vigilance. His boot moved on a loose stone and Linda swung round. She identified him instantly, was swiftly by his side.

'Tex, there's a guy down there, maybe one of the Kid's outfit . . . I thought I'd got him but then I saw him move again. I reckon. . . .'

Tex got there, then. She'd mistaken him for a bandit, had laid for him. The Kid hadn't left anyone to guard his flanks. Tex got there, up to a point, but he still didn't know how she came to be on the scene at all. The last he had seen of her she had been vamoosing down the trail away from the pass.

'You were layin' for me,' he said, and then was interrupted by a voice behind him.

'Get your hands up.'

Tex had forgotten the two guys held-up on the trail. Now, as he turned, he saw one of them, the giant, standing there with a gun in his hand. The other materialized from nearby, also with a gun.

'Reckon they forgot to lift the rods from the ponies,' grunted the first guy. 'OK Linda, get away from him. You're OK now, nothin' to worry about, I got him covered.'

Tex had put up his Colt when Linda had recognized him, but he wasn't worrying. A mistake had been made, the second in a short space of time, or more accurately the third counting Tex's error in thinking one of the Kid's hoodlums was laying for him. Linda could clear it up without any fuss.

She did so at once.

'Cut it out, Jeb, this guy is all right. . . . I met up with him earlier along the trail. We heard the shots, I reckon that was when the Kid first laid for you, and he got movin' to lend a hand.' Then, as the man called Jeb hesitated, she spoke again. 'Put up your gun, I tell you Mister Scarron is OK.'

Jeb grunted but then did as he was told, putting up his gun. His companion followed suit. Watching him Tex decided that not often before had he seen any guy who looked more like a rat. At closer quarters he could see that his skin was a dirty grey, that the eyes were narrow and closely set on either side of his nose, that his lips were thin. For all that he was so much smaller than Jeb, Tex reckoned he was about twice as dangerous.

'I don't get any o' this,' he said now. 'We got held-up by the Kid, there ain't no doubt who the guy was, an' then. . . .'

'I'll give you the facts, Snake,' interrupted the girl. 'I met up with Mister Scarron, he's on his way to the Bar X, Dave Brand is his uncle. We heard the shots and Mister Scarron got movin'. I followed along,' she added, with a swift, sidelong glance at Tex. 'I don't aim usually to be left out of things. I saw you two held-up and then I sighted another guy lyin' up. I thought he was a hoodlum so I tried to get him. But I made a mistake – it was Mister Scarron.'

Tex tilted back his Stetson. So that was it; Linda had foxed him, he reckoned she'd not intended to clear but had bluffed him. She had followed along and the result was that the Kid and his buddy had got away.

'Sorry, I slipped up badly,' said the girl, who didn't need to be a thought-reader to guess what Tex was thinking.

Jeb Callahan accepted the explanation and nodded at Tex.

'Mighty good of you to do what you could, stranger,' he grunted. 'I guess me an' Snake are grateful, that right, Snake?'

'Sure . . . I guess we'll get back to the River. The Parson won't stand for a guy like the Kid rustlin' in on this territory.' Jeb ran a huge hand over his unshaven jaw.

'That's right . . . the Kid lifted five hundred dollars off us, that ain't so good.'

'You talkin' about Parson Dean?' he asked. 'You know him?'

It was Linda who answered. Sure Jeb and Snake knew the Parson. Jeb was foreman at the Double K, the ranch owned by the Parson, who was also proprietor of the hotel at Grant's River and of several other concerns, as Tex was to discover later, Snake was one of his employees, too.

'That's mighty interestin',' drawled Tex. He wanted to know all he could about the Parson, and not merely from Sam Steel. He wanted the set-up from every angle. He wanted to meet up with the Parson, too, and the sooner the better. It was an idea to make the encounter before he talked to Sam. 'Sure, mighty interestin',' he repeated. 'I've heard of the Parson . . . a pretty big guy in these parts they tell me?'

Jeb's face tightened just for a moment. He wasn't too good at concealing his feelings Tex reckoned. But it was the man Snake who answered, swiftly and smoothly.

'That's right, mister, a pretty big man.' And then, 'Where'd you hear about him?'

Ted shrugged, answering vaguely. He'd heard talk at Indian Creek, in the hotel there, that was all.

'Guess I'll come with you to Grant's River,' he added. 'I'd sure like to meet the Parson, he sounds like a good guy and one worth knowin'.'

As he spoke he was conscious of tension. Jeb was staring at him, eyes narrowed; Snake's face was blank but he couldn't avoid giving away that he, too, was wondering what lay behind the suggestion – that was the way Tex reckoned it out. Remembering what Sam had said in his letter, knowing now that Jeb and Snake were employed by Parson Dean, he didn't have much difficulty in working out what these two guys were thinking. Linda had told them that he was on his way to the Bar X, that Dave Brand was his uncle. They were wondering just what was the reason for his visit.

Snake provided some corroborative evidence for this guesswork.

'You're goin' to the Bar X?' he asked slowly, and when Tex nodded, 'Sure . . . you come along with us, mister. I reckon the Parson will be glad to meet you.'

Corroborative evidence it was, Tex reckoned, this reference to the Bar X. There was something else he was pretty sure about. The tension, which had now passed, almost as quickly as it had arisen, was not confined to Jeb and Snake. Linda had said nothing, but Tex was aware that she was standing there rigid. He reckoned that the talk of Parson Dean interested her, far more than the occasion seemed to warrant.

He remembered her own reference to the Parson, which didn't link up with what Sam had told him in the letter. It didn't link up, either, with the employment of two guys whom Tex, out of his long experience, judged to be dangerous and crooked – especially Snake – and though as yet he hadn't met Parson Dean, what he'd heard about him didn't lead him to think that the big man of Grant's River was a sucker either. In turn that meant that the Parson knew that these two guys of his weren't to be trusted much farther than they could be seen.

Tex didn't know where he was yet, but already, after so short a time in the River district, he was even more interested in his mission than he had been. There were cross-currents.

There was the Kid, for instance. It seemed certain that the notorious bandit was an extra on the scene. For one thing he had moved into the area only very recently according to reports; for another he had laid for two of the Parson's men. He couldn't on the face of it have any connection with the Parson's set-up, but on the other hand

... on the other hand Tex was thinking right now of something which had been nibbling at the back of his mind ever since he had come on Linda Forbes laying for him.

Her story had been plausible enough, on the surface, but there were two points troubling Tex. Remembering the lie of the country he reckoned she must have come via the defile. In that case she must have seen his pony tethered by the side of the trail. Second she had known that he had ridden that way and was aiming to investigate the shooting. The two put together worried him. She had known he was around, but she had assumed without query that a third bandit was lurking amongst the rocks, hadn't apparently wondered whether it could be Tex himself. Her intervention had resulted in the Kid and his buddy escaping.

What reason could she have for intervening on behalf of a bandit? And anyway if so it didn't link with her good opinion of the Parson and the obvious fact that these two guys of his knew her well and were friendly with her.

Tex spoke again, ostensibly to Snake, but with an eye on Linda.

'I guess I don't like lettin' a guy like the Kid slip me,' he drawled. 'I've been up against hoodlums before, and they ain't got away. I reckon I'm goin' to get the Kid if he stays around here.'

He saw, or thought he saw, the girl tense again; but the moment was so brief that he couldn't be sure. When she spoke her voice was normal.

'I wish you luck . . . I'll come down to the River, too, Jeb. Buck is down there at the hotel and I can join up with him.'

'OK Linda, like you say,' grunted Jeb. 'We'll be movin'.'

Linda had left her pony not far from where Tex had tethered his beast, proof that she must have passed and seen the animal. He noted the fact but said nothing; and neither did she. A little while later the four of them rode down to Grant's River.

CHAPTER 3

Parson Dean, thus nicknamed with the sardonic humour of the West, for he was about as unlike a clergyman, both in appearance and habits as any man could be, sat at his desk in the private office of the Grant's River Hotel. A cigar, half-smoked, was gripped by his firm white teeth, set between full, fleshy lips; without removing the cigar he drew at it strongly while engaged in the occupation which pleased him the most. His little eyes, pillowed in folds of flesh, gleamed as his thick fingers rustled the piles of dollar bills on the desk.

The Parson was counting his money, for today was pay-day, the first of a calendar month. It was the day when the Parson was paid off; the day when ranchers of the Grant's River territory paid out. The piles of bills on the desk were imposing.

Shifting his plump body the Parson reached for a ledger, being careful when he placed it on the desk not to cover the gun which lay there ready to his hand. Parson Dean rarely took risks; never when he was checking over the contributions to the mutual protection society, a criminal racket which though flourishing in many large cities was a new one in ranching country. The gun was loaded and cocked.

Near at hand was a window which gave on to Main Street, the principal thoroughfare of the dilapidated, unsalubrious township of Grant's River. The place had sweltered through the hot day; at this time of night, for it was gone eleven o'clock, it lay uneasily under the moon, lit also here and there by patches of brilliant naphtha light.

The hotel, enjoying one of its peak hours, was spilling out a broad splash of light on to the sidewalk and the dusty street which was really only a continuation of the trail running down from the Black Hills pass. The gambling saloon not far away was also illuminated – and full of ranchers and cowhands busy losing money. Farther down Main Street was another drinking establishment, like the hotel and the gambling joint, owned by the Parson. It was at this secondary saloon that Dean kept the women he had imported into Grant's River to attend to the pleasures of the husky cowhands, and incidentally bring him more profit.

Even in the deceptive light of the moon and the naphtha flares, the township was hardly attractive. It consisted only of Main Street, lined with wooden buildings weatherbeaten and stained, the paint peeling off all those which were not owned by the Parson. Behind the buildings stretched waste ground, with here and there shacks rising, with heaps of debris and rubbish which attracted flies and gave off an aroma to which the inhabitants had become accustomed but which did not attract strangers.

Not by any standard was Grant's River a pleasant spot, but it suited the Parson well enough. It was the centre of a rich ranching country where there was money, a district moreover where the ranchers formed a self-contained community cut off from the rest of Arizona by natural boundaries, with a tradition of keeping themselves to themselves. Arizona itself, until very recently, had been governed by a man slack enough to suit the Parson's ends.

He had alighted upon Grant's River five years before and had struck lucky, very lucky. As a result of that stroke of fortune he'd brought Jeb Callahan over the border from Mexico and a tough bunch of hoodlums, including the man Snake, had been recruited. The Double K had been bought, the mutual protection racket started. As profits increased the hotel and the other concerns had been purchased. The territory was being systematically milked. At first it had been hard going, but after a bit of initial trouble the set-up had made out.

There came a knock at the door. The Parson's hand closed over the butt of his gun.

'Who is it?'

'Poston. . . .'

The Parson pushed back his chair and lumbered to the door. His bald head gleamed grotesquely under the light of the swinging oil-lamp. He didn't rely on his appearance to persuade others to accept his leadership, and it was fortunate for him that he didn't need to, for his fat, often jovial face gave no clue to the ruthless purpose which lurked in him. He relied on personality and deeds.

Sheriff Poston, a nondescript guy of middle-age, whom the Parson had experienced no difficulty in buying, came into the room when the door was unlocked.

'No sign o' Brand yet,' he stated. 'He's runnin' it late, ain't he?'

The Parson went back to the desk, ruffled the pages, stared at one headed *Dave Brand, Bar X.* When he looked up at Poston again his little eyes were like pebbles, opaque and dangerous.

'Sure . . . if he don't come I reckon we'll have to see him.'

The Sheriff fingered the brim of his Stetson. Nobody ever entered the Parson's private office without uncovering.

'How, boss?'

'How? What you mean? I'll put the boys on to his joint and prove he needs protection. It's been quite a while since I had to do that to any o' the guys around here, maybe Brand has forgotten what happened to those I attended to at the beginnin'.'

The sheriff said nothing for a bit, but obviously he was uneasy. Subordinates in any organization are usually conditioned by their superior. Poston was no exception. The Governor of Arizona had for years been slack and they whispered corrupt; Poston, his subordinate, took after him. What was good enough, or bad enough, for the Governor, was OK by Poston of Grant's River. The Parson had bought him three years before. That had been an essential step in setting up his racket.

But now the man who nominally was sheriff, though he took his orders from the real boss of the territory, shuffled his feet and looked ill at ease.

'Well, what's biting you?' snarled the Parson.

'I guess maybe we ought to lay off,' was the muttered reply. 'They say this new guy, York, is a go-getter, aimin' to clean-up. I don't reckon I want any trouble that'll bring him down here.'

The other drew back his thick lips. He'd noticed a change in manner ever since it had become known that York had taken over as Governor. Poston was a rat, and like a rat easily scared.

'Cut it out. There ain't no danger, this guy York has got plenty to do without interferin' with us . . . we're quite a way from Phoenix.' He paused and then added with meaning, 'And if there is danger, I guess it ain't nothin' compared with what there'll be for you if you don't do what you're told, Poston . . . understand?'

Poston did understand. He was remembering the times when at the beginning of Dean's operations, when he'd first started his mutual protection society, he'd proved just how ruthless and dangerous he could be. The ranchers had laughed at the idea of a guy rustling in on the territory setting up a cock-eyed society and demanding subscriptions from property owners to finance the set-up he proposed starting to protect members from bandits and hoodlums. They hadn't laughed long, not after two ranches were burned down, a third was robbed, cattle were rustled and one guy was murdered. All that the Parson had done, with the aid of his hired gang. He'd proved that the territory needed protection. After that the ranchers had come round. Now the Parson ran the district – and there was no trouble so long as the dues were paid on the first day of each month.

Poston was remembering. He hastened to make his peace.

'Aw, boss, I didn't mean nothin', I only thought maybe . . .'

'Don't think, buddy, I'll do that for you. If Dave Brand don't pay up I'll look after him.' Then, after a slight pause, during which he packed up the dollars and put them in the heavy safe, he turned back to the sheriff. 'What's this about the Kid rustlin' in?' he asked. 'What you know 'bout it?'

'Nothin', boss. I don't reckon there's anythin' in it. The Kid knows you're runnin' this area, I guess, he wouldn't take the risk o' ridin' this way. Some folk'll say anythin'.'

Parson Dean grunted. Maybe Poston was right; but maybe he was wrong. The Parson had heard as much about the Kid as anyone. He didn't under-rate him. If he took it into his head to come to the River district, if he was already here, there'd be trouble. Dean wasn't standing for interference, nor for cutting two ways with any other guy. The Kid worked alone or with not more than one buddy, it was said. OK he'd find himself outnumbered – if he came.

The Parson glanced out of the window. Jeb and Snake were due by now. What the heck was keeping them?

He didn't know it but though there didn't seem to be any connection between their absence and the notorious Kid, no reason why he should have thought of them so quickly after talking of the Kid, there was a link all right. Maybe Parson Dean was telepathic without realizing it.

Poston didn't know anything about Jeb or Snake. He had something else on his mind, to him of more importance.

'Reckon I came for my cut, boss,' he muttered. 'I can do with it.'

There was one thing about Dean – he never stalled when it came to paying out. He'd found that it was to his advantage to keep his assistants happy. Poston was on his pay-roll; today was pay-day, for others as well as for himself.

He went back to the safe, swung open the door and reached for the packet of dollars put aside ready. As he did so his eyes rested for a moment on a heavy steel box which contained exactly fifty per cent of the last quarter's profits from the various concerns, including the mutual protection society. A flicker of emotion crossed the Parson's face as he looked at the box; then it was wiped away. He picked up the small wad of bills and relocked the safe.

'Here's your cut, Poston. Now get out . . . if you see those two guys o' mine, tell 'em to get down here pronto.'

The sheriff cleared, tucking the dollars into his pocket. The more dough he had the more he needed. The Parson watched him go with a sardonic expression in his eyes. He knew that most of the money would find its way back into the safe via the gambling tables. Poston was a heavy gambler. Most nights he was down at the joint; and most nights he lost.

When he'd gone the Parson went back to the desk, sat there smoking, staring out of the window. Part of his mind was occupied with Dave Brand, owner of the Bar X; with the fact that Brand hadn't yet shown up to pay his dues as a member of the mutual protection society. Maybe he was aimin' to make trouble? The Parson blew a long streamer of smoke . . . and dismissed the idea of Dave getting above himself. He was running to seed and letting the Bar X run downhill badly. According to what the Parson had heard Dave had been pretty tough in the old days, before his wife had died. Well, maybe he had been tough, but he wasn't that way now. He wasn't the guy to go looking for trouble. There'd be no showdown with him. He'd pay up all right.

The Parson dismissed the subject. His glance travelled to the safe . . . now he was thinking about the steel box with the dollars inside, thinking also about the stroke of luck he'd had when he first came to Grant's River. But he wasn't so sure now that it had been such good luck; or rather that he hadn't already paid highly enough for it. It was a thought which had occupied him more and more lately, growing stronger.

He was sitting pretty here at Grant's River. He didn't pay any attention to the rumours that the new man, York, was a go-getter. Arizona was a mighty big state; it would take a long time for York to get around to Grant's River, even if he ever did. There was no reason why he should. Poston was OK and on the surface the mutual protection set-up was legal enough. There was no law that said guys weren't allowed to band together to protect themselves or spend their own dollars hiring unofficial bodyguards. There was maybe a law that stated ranches shouldn't be burned down, sheriffs bribed or guys murdered, but there was no proof any of these crimes had been committed.

The Parson wasn't worrying about the new Governor. He wasn't worrying about Dave Brand or the Kid, either. He was sitting pretty all right . . . his worry was concerned with whether he couldn't work it that he made even more dough. He reckoned the time had come to do something about that fifty per cent of the profits lying there in the safe.

After a bit he stubbed out his cigar and left the room. Across the narrow passage outside was a door leading into the saloon, now full, with a piano blaring. The Parson passed this door and moved down the passage to another room. He stood for a few moments unnoticed in the doorway, watching the card players hunched round a table.

Facing him was Buck Forbes of the Lazy Y, a smart, youngish guy, smart in his own estimation that was. He was sitting now, his attention entirely concentrated on the cards, his sharp, foxy face slightly flushed. The Parson noticed that his hands were trembling ever so slightly.

He was a guy who bluffed nobody but himself. He reckoned he was pretty good at poker. The more he lost down here at the hotel or in the gambling joint the more he cursed his luck. It never occurred to him that the cards might be stacked.

The Parson waited, watching. Two minutes later Buck's hand was down. He had four kings, just about what the Parson had reckoned.

'Guess that's OK?' said the young man, face now even more flushed. 'I reckon that'll pay me back for what I've lost tonight.'

All but Spike had thrown in. Spike's sallow face exhibited no emotion whatever.

'Your mistake, Buck,' he drawled.

He showed his hand – it was a straight flush with the ace high.

Buck Forbes stared at the cards and then abruptly pushed back his chair.

'Heck, this ain't my lucky night.'

'You'll make up tomorrow maybe,' murmured Spike. 'Want another?'

Then he saw the Parson and swivelled round in his chair. The others looked up but said nothing. They were guys who did as they were told.

'Want us, boss?' asked Spike.

'Sure, I've been expectin' Jeb and Snake, but they ain't turned up. I reckon maybe you'd best get up to the ranch, Spike and find out . . .'

He was interrupted by hurrying footsteps on the bare boards of the passage outside and then in the doorway appeared Rocky Schultz, about the quickest guy with a throwing knife anywhere in the cow-country. He was small and lithe and in spite of his name with more than a drop of Mexican blood in his veins.

'Say, boss, Jeb and Snake have shown up.. . . .'

The Parson grunted. That was OK then, Spike needn't go up to the Double K.

His satisfaction didn't last long, though. Rocky was talking again, hurriedly.

'Boss, they met up with the Kid on the trail . . . the bum held 'em up, lifted five hundred dollars.'

There was a stunned silence in the room. Spike, by now on his feet, stood by the table staring unbelievingly at Rocky. The other three stopped fiddling with the cards, faces blank with astonishment. Buck Forbes forgot about how much dough he'd lost.

The Parson himself broke the pause. He took a step forward and grabbed Rocky.

'What you givin' me?' he rasped. 'I ain't in the mood for jokes, Rocky.'

'It ain't no joke, boss. I tell you Jeb an' Snake got held up by the Kid. Jeb says there ain't no doubt it was the Kid. If it hadn't been for some guy called Scarron maybe they'd have been bumped off . . . and the skirt was there, too.'

'The skirt? What skirt?'

'Linda . . .'

At that Buck moved. He thought a mighty lot of himself did Buck. He wasn't having any cowhand talking about his cousin this way. His gun appeared in his hand as he moved across the room.

'You can cut that out,' he snapped. 'You talk respectful . . . Linda ain't no skirt and to you I reckon she's Miss Forbes.'

The Parson turned on him, face dangerous.

'Put up that rod, Buck, don't you start no trouble here, it looks like I've got enough. I got somethin' better to do than listen to kid's stuff from you.'

Rocky Schultz grimaced, his leathery face puckish.

'That's right, boss, you got to think about the other Kid's stuff, I guess.'

The Parson was in no mood for this sort of play with words. He put out an arm and brushed Rocky aside.

'Where's Jeb?' he demanded. And then, as he reached the door he swung back on Rocky, remembering something. 'What's that you said about a stranger? Who is this guy Scarron?'

It wasn't Rocky who answered. The Parson heard footsteps in the passage and turned back to the door again. A man came into view who had evidently heard the last question.

'I reckon I'm Scarron,' he drawled, 'Tex they call me. You the guy they call the Parson? I'm mighty glad to meet you.'

CHAPTER 4

Tex took in the Parson, the fleshy face, the little eyes, the grotesquely bald head, the false appearance of joviality. It didn't look like Tex was summing him up, his eyes seemed casual, but there wasn't much eluded his gaze. One thing that he didn't miss was something that lurked behind the Parson's little eyes set in the folds of flesh; that something Tex Scarron reckoned spelled danger. Here was a guy who in spite of his appearance was ruthless, probably a killer.

The newcomer to Grant's River had met killers before. He'd discovered pretty soon in his haphazard career riding around the place looking for trouble that a killer can come out in all shapes and sizes. There wasn't a killer's face. That could be anything. In his time Tex had met guys who looked as though they wouldn't hurt a fly but in fact had been murderers. There wasn't such a thing as a typical killer's face, but there were killer's eyes. This Parson Dean had those eyes.

'Sure, I guess you must be the Parson,' repeated Tex. 'I'm glad to meet you . . . I've heard about you.'

In his turn Dean surveyed Tex Scarron. A hard-bitten hombre this, he reckoned, tough and probably quick with his gun. He'd been around. Like Tex, the Parson had learned to judge men . . . and he, too, recognized danger when he saw it. This visitor was dangerous.

They summed each other up but neither of them gave anything

away. Then the Parson nodded.

'I'm Parson Dean,' he grunted. 'Rocky says you cut in to help my boys with the Kid. That right, stranger?'

'Better ask them,' was the reply, Tex jerking his head at Jeb and Snake.

The Parson turned to Jeb. His voice wasn't pleasant when he spoke.

'Well, what about it? Rocky says the Kid held you up.'

Jeb shifted his feet uneasily. For all that he was a huge man, who could have broken the Parson in two, he cowered before the expression in the boss's little eyes. Jeb, like a tiger menaced by the personality of his trainer, was scared of the Parson – which made him a valuable tool.

'Aw, boss, it wasn't our fault,' he muttered. 'We wasn't expectin' anythin' like that. We was ridin' back from the Creek with the dough an' the guy came out at us with an-other hombre. He stuck us up, boss. . . .'

The Parson's thick lips drew back over his teeth.

'He stuck you up! What you reckon you are, a couple o' old women? Or maybe you don't carry rods around with you any more? Reckon you've gone yellow, Jeb.'

Jeb glowered, but before he could answer this charge Snake broke in. He wasn't scared of the Parson, not the way Jeb was, although he obeyed orders – or had done up to now.

'It ain't no good talkin' like that, boss. The Kid had us all jammed up, got us covered 'fore we could draw. You ain't heard the lot yet. We didn't let him take the dough easy . . . we made a break for it an' got our rods out. But I guess the Kid is pretty slick.'

Tex knew what had happened for Jeb and Snake had talked on the way to Grant's River. They'd made a break for it after the Kid had held them up, had got at their guns and shots had been exchanged. But the Kid had ducked down behind cover and then had pulled a fast one, getting round behind the Double K boys while his companion held their attention from the front. The Kid had got the drop on them properly the second time, which was just before Tex himself had come up.

Now he listened to the tale recounted yet again but only with half an ear. He was watching the Parson – and keeping an eye on the others as well. The Parson was a killer; he reckoned the other three Double K hands in the room weren't much better. He'd walked into a tough set-up all right.

The other guy had a look of Linda about him. It didn't take much skill to work out that this was probably Buck Forbes, of the Lazy Y. The girl had said he was down here at the hotel. Tex's eyes flicked over the table, noted the cards lying there. It seemed like Buck had been playing poker. Tex hoped he knew what he was doing . . . he was sure the others did.

That the guy was indeed Buck Forbes was proved when he pushed forward, interrupting the tale Jeb and Snake were telling.

'Where's my cousin?' he demanded. 'Rocky said she was up there on the trail.'

It was Tex who answered.

'She's OK mister, met a friend in Main Street and gone with him . . . a guy called Dwight, seems he owns the newssheet.'

Buck grunted. He knew Pop Dwight, everyone in the district did. He owned the *River Gazette*, writing it up and printing it every week pretty well single-handed.

'What was she doin' up on the trail?' he demanded.

Tex shrugged his shoulders.

'It ain't no good askin' me. I guess you're the one who ought to be makin' sure she don't ride around the place gettin' mixed up in trouble.'

Buck's hand fell to the butt of his gun.

'You got a nerve, stranger, comin' here tellin' me what I ought to do. I reckon I don't . . .'

Tex didn't move, though if he'd had to he could have beaten Buck to the draw even though he had some leeway to make up. But as it was the Parson took over.

His hand closed over Buck's gun wrist like a vice.

'Cut it out,' he snarled. 'You know Linda does what she likes and

I guess you know you ought to stop her ridin' around alone.' Then to Tex, 'Don't you take no notice of him, he don't always mean what he says.'

Buck Forbes glowered, but he made no further aggressive move.

By now the Parson knew what had happened up on the trail. He knew that Jeb and Snake had lost five hundred dollars; he was willing to accept that the hoodlum who had held them up, with the help of another masked guy, was the Kid. The description fitted and so did the slickness exhibited. Jeb and Snake weren't exactly chickens, but they'd been taken for a ride. It was long odds that the bandit had been the Kid.

'Too bad about the dough, boss,' muttered Jeb, 'but we did our best. We got it off Hackamore all right, down at the Creek, he parted OK an' we was bringin' it back when . . .'

The Parson interrupted him swiftly.

'Sure he parted, those steers were worth five hundred dollars. OK you'd best come to the office.'

Tex saw the expression which crossed Jeb's broad face and he knew that the Parson was bluffing. Whoever Hackamore was and whatever he'd paid over the money for, it wasn't in payment for steers purchased. In view of Sam Steel's letter Tex didn't have a lot of difficulty in working out why the money had been paid.

The Parson turned back to the newcomer.

'I guess it was mighty good of you to take a hand, Scarron,' he said. 'I'm grateful . . . but I reckon that skirt wants a belt taken to her like I said,' with a malicious glance at Buck Forbes. 'And don't you start in tellin' me she ain't no skirt,' he added, as Buck opened his mouth. 'I reckon I say what I want, and any guy who don't like it knows what to do about it. OK Jeb, and you Snake, get goin'.'

Buck Forbes, who was about twenty-seven, Tex judged, glared at the Parson but he made no sort of move. He was angry all right, but he was something else as well – scared of the Parson. Tex was dead sure of that, he'd seen too many men in too many moods to make a mistake. The Parson had him where he wanted him. Just why Tex didn't know, but maybe he'd find out.

When the Parson had gone, after telling Tex he'd be back to talk to him again pretty soon and that in the meantime drinks were on the house, Buck perceptibly relaxed. And relaxing got brave, now the Parson was gone.

'I guess no guy tells me what to do,' he muttered. 'I'll look after Linda, I don't need nobody to give me orders.'

A bartender brought in liquor. Tex took a glass of beer and drained it down. His throat was dry and the beer was welcome. Having met Linda Forbes and now Buck, he didn't reckon there was much chance of the young man persuading the girl to do anything she didn't want to do, or stop doing what she wanted to do. Buck, he estimated, was a guy who was about ten per cent as smart as he thought he was, with about as many guts as would go on a dime piece. He could talk but that was about all.

Tex knew a whole lot more now than he had done when he left Indian Creek. Some of what he knew he had been told – as for instance that Linda was an orphan and that Buck had no father, living at the Lazy Y with his mother who was an invalid; a good bit he'd discovered by using his eyes and his ears. Buck Forbes was mixed up with the Parson set-up, was scared of the Parson. Linda had given Dean a good character, and if she'd pulled a fast one up on the trail, gunning for the Kid, not against him, that also surely meant she wasn't playing for the Parson. There were cross-currents.

Spike Warren jerked his head at the cards.

'Ain't you goin' to play again, Buck?' he asked. 'If your cousin is with Pop, I reckon she'll be a long time yet.'

Buck hesitated but then went to the table.

'I'll play,' he grunted. 'I reckon the luck's got to change some time.'

Tex, watching Spike's slim fingers busy shuffling the cards, wasn't so sure about that. He'd seen a good few sharpers at work in his time.

'How 'bout me cuttin' in?' he asked.

'OK stranger, you can cut in.'

Tex sat down, watching Spike deal. He watched with interest but didn't seem to. Nothing about him indicated that he'd learned all the tricks at the feet of Jesse Smith, reckoned to be the slickest sharper anywhere east of the Atlantic. Tex wasn't giving away anything – not yet.

The other Double K boys took up their cards and play started. Tex deliberately played the sort of game he thought was expected of him. Spike wasn't so hot at first and neither were his buddies . . . Buck began to win. He didn't win heavily, but he won, enough to encourage him. Let the sucker win a bit, at first – that was the golden rule employed by sharpers all over the world.

Gradually Tex changed his tactics, began to bet more heavily, after he'd won once. He gave it away when he was holding a good hand, knowing that Spike and the others, with the exception of Buck, who didn't count, would pick up the signs and read them correctly. Tex was preparing the ground.

He knew by now that without a doubt the deck was stacked when Spike or the other Double K boys dealt. It was stacked very cleverly and Buck hadn't a suspicion; but Tex had more than a suspicion. Jesse Smith had taught him that trick of stacking the cards, in return for a favour of a different sort. He'd taught him something else, too, a trick worth two of the one these crooks were employing.

By the time Tex was ready to pull his coup Buck had lost all he'd made at the beginning and a whole lot more as well. Tex himself had lost fifty dollars. He'd been framed on the last hand, he knew that, but it suited his purpose. He'd been dealt cards good enough to tempt him to plunge – which obligingly he'd done. He'd lost to Spike as he knew he would. But that was OK. What he did now looked natural enough, he hoped.

He dug into his pocket and brought out a hundred dollars, counting them carefully, watched by Spike and the others.

'I got a feelin' the luck's goin' to change,' he said. 'The cards have been gettin' better . . . my deal, ain't it?'

He took the cards and shuffled them. Spike's face was a blank, but Tex reckoned he knew what he was thinking. Here was a sucker who thought the luck was building up for him . . . he'd soon find out his mistake.

Tex shuffled, apparently exactly as he had shuffled in previous rounds. The Double K boys were fly but by this time they reckoned Tex was a mug and about as dangerous as Buck Forbes. But even if they'd thought different they wouldn't have seen Tex stack the deck. Jesse Smith had taught him well. He didn't make a false move. By the time he'd dealt he knew what each man was holding; and he knew the order of the cards in the rest of the pack.

It worked out all right. After a couple of rounds the other three Double K boys dropped out. Buck stuck it for a bit but then he packed up. That left Tex and Spike in. Spike was holding four kings, which he must take as a stroke of luck, for when Tex or Buck was dealing the game was on the level. The chances of Tex holding anything better than the four kings was about a million to one against.

Tex played his part pretty well; letting his excitement peep out from his eyes, he indicated by a slight trembling of his hands as the pool mounted. He hoped that Spike would work it out that he was holding maybe four queens.

Spike raised him and the pool stood at three hundred dollars. Tex stared at him, then back at his cards. He seemed to hesitate; then he brought out more dough, raised the pool again.

Spike drew at his cigarette. Tex fumbled, dropped a card face up on the table, grabbed it swiftly, but not too swiftly. Spike saw it all right, a queen. Tex hoped that would persuade him to raise again.

It did. Spike reckoned he was sitting pretty. With four queens this newcomer thought he was set to grab the pool.

Tex raised again, so did Spike. When it was Tex's turn once more he decided that the time had come to call it off.

'I'm cleaned out,' he muttered. 'OK pal . . .'

Spike turned up his cards, four kings as Tex had known.

'I guess that's good enough,' drawled Spike, and stretched out his hand for the pool, now worth five hundred dollars. Tex said abruptly.

'Hold it . . . what about this?'

He turned up his own cards, a straight flush in spades, ace high.

'I guess we're playin' ace high,' said Tex.

Spike let fall an oath. Then he came to his feet and at the same time his hand reached for his gun. As he grabbed at the butt Tex's gun was out, covering him.

'Not this time, pal,' drawled Tex. 'Get your hand away from that rod . . . I guess I mean it.'

One of the others, a little guy, jerked forward, the table was swept against Tex's legs. He grabbed at the back of his chair to steady himself but Spike seized his chance. He lurched at Tex, got a grip and the next moment there was uproar, Spike's buddies piling in.

In the midst of the fight the door was flung open and there was the Parson, a gun in his hand.

'Break it up,' he ground, 'break it up.'

He was obeyed. Tex was now disarmed, his gun fallen to the floor. He stood there looking into the barrel of the Parson's gun. Behind the Parson was Jeb, another guy Tex hadn't seen before . . . and Linda Forbes.

'What goes on?' snarled the Parson. 'I ain't standin' for trouble here.'

'We was playin' poker, boss . . . this guy pulled a fast one, reckon he took us for suckers. He stacked the deck.'

Tex said nothing. He didn't like looking into the wrong end of a gun. Talking could wait for a bit; he was working out how to grab the Parson's rod.

Then Linda moved, pushed past Jeb and came into the room. The table was on its side now, the cards scattered on the floor. She stooped down swiftly and picked up two.

'What you know about this?' she asked, holding up the cards. 'I guess it's a queer sort of pack with two aces of spades in it.'

Tex narrowed his eyes. He'd rigged the deck all right, but not by using two aces. In the commotion Spike or one of the other boys must have dropped the second ace. It, and maybe other useful cards, had been parked somewhere handy. Reckoning he had a cast-iron hand on the level, Spike hadn't troubled to try any palming.

'I don't know nothin' about it,' said Tex. 'What do you think, that I came with another pack on me lookin' the same as the one used here? That don't work out, I reckon.'

Linda looked at Spike Warren.

'I reckon you got two packs lookin' the same? Sure you have, and this guy grabbed one when you weren't lookin', that's how it was worked. I reckon we can do without a sharper at the River.'

Buck, who had lost a packet on the last hand, before he dropped out, agreed with her.

'Sure, let's run him out o' town, boys.' Then, as an after-thought, 'Or maybe the sheriff could lock him up for a bit to cool his heels.'

Sheriff Poston, the guy Tex hadn't recognized, shuffled his feet, looking at the Parson obviously for instructions. By now Tex knew that he didn't stand a chance of pulling a fast one. If he'd moved quickly at the beginning he might have managed, but then Linda had found the two aces and that had sidetracked him long enough to let the chance slip. Others had crowded into the room now, including the thickset, stocky Pop Dwight, middle-aged with a mass of grey hair and printer's ink on his hands. He didn't have a gun out but others had by now.

They came at him and Tex had more sense than put up a fight against such odds. He let them grab him. He was in for a beating-up, he reckoned, but he had to take it.

As he was hustled out of the room he glimpsed Linda Forbes standing watching. She'd landed him in for this, that was certain, had suggested that they could do without him at the River. But right now there was something in her eyes as she watched him taken out that didn't link with what she'd done. There was fear, and Tex reckoned it wasn't fear for herself.

But Tex wasn't given any chance to think much about it or try to work it out. He was dragged from the room and along the passage to a door which gave on to Main Street. His other gun had been grabbed and he was helpless, disarmed and outnumbered. He'd run into bad trouble all right.

CHAPTER 5

There was no chance of making a break for it yet. By the time Tex was hustled out into Main Street his original captors had been greatly increased, for from the saloon itself had poured a mass of cowhands and loafers once they knew something was cooking. Word was passed round that here was a guy who had come busting into Grant's River aiming to hijack, and by the time the information reached the outermost fringes of the mob it had become garbled so that half the crowd reckoned that here was a bandit caught red-handed.

Not only the information became garbled but the intention to run him out of town altered – and ominously altered. Arizona as a whole was not noted for its law-abiding habits; this small section of the state had always gone its own way, using its own methods. Some guy at the back of the mob raised the cry of lynching.

'String him up!'

It was seized on by others. Those who weren't drunk with liquor were effected by the mob instinct, which can make men drunk in another way and just as dangerous. The words were picked up, repeated, flung towards the centre of the crowd where Tex Scarron was now roughly tied up.

'Lynch the guy! String him up!'

Tex knew he was in about as bad a spot of trouble as any that had come his way in a life which had not lacked danger. When the cry of lynching was taken up, amid a roar of approval, he felt something trickle down his spin he'd never felt before – the cold chill of fear. Odds up to a certain point he didn't mind. To be outnumbered by as much as twenty to one, when he had a gun in his hand, couldn't scare Tex, but this was different. There were not only a good fifty tough guys milling round him, but they were in the grip of mob fever.

The Parson wasn't on view, and neither was the sheriff. They'd stayed behind in the hotel. No doubt Dean knew he could leave matters in the hands of the mob; and the sheriff maybe didn't want to know what happened, not officially. But Buck Forbes was there, along with Jeb and Snake, with Spike Warren, the guy they called Rocky Schultz and the other three Double K boys who had been playing poker. It was Buck who now took charge.

'Sure, we'll string him up,' he shouted. 'OK Jeb, get movin' with him.'

Jeb's lips drew back in a jagged grin.

'Sure . . . get him on his horse.'

They hoisted Tex on to his pony, and his wrists were tied behind his back.

The mob, grabbing their own beasts, followed along. Buck set Tex's pony going at a canter. Tex rolled round in the saddle, his feet hanging clear of the stirrups. He looked back at the cowhands streaming after him, their guns out, raising whoopee, not much caring about the rights or wrongs of the business but only out for blood. It had only needed the lynching cry to be raised to bring this crowd to a fever pitch of blood lust. Tomorrow, maybe, most of them would regret what they'd done, but that wouldn't help Tex if by then he was swinging free in the wind, strung up from some tree.

He hadn't reckoned on landing himself in a jam like this; and if he had known he was destined to be the victim of mob violence he wouldn't have banked on thinking about a woman – or rather a girl – while he was on his way to his death. But that was what he was doing as he was taken down Main Street. Linda Forbes had seemed OK once they'd had their show-down up near the pass. He'd realized that some of the things she'd said and done didn't link up, maybe provided evidence that she wasn't on the level, but he hadn't said anything about that and reckoned he hadn't given it away by his manner. But now she'd turned on him.

He had her to thank for what was happening right now. He hadn't a doubt now that she had deliberately laid for him at the hotel; he didn't believe that the suggestion that he should be run out of town had been made on impulse. She had laid for him all right, had used her wits and had reckoned that all she had to do then was leave it to the boys to get shot of him.

Sure, but had she banked on what was happening now? Tex didn't reckon so. He remembered the expression on her face and in her eyes when he'd been hustled from the room down at the hotel, when maybe for the first time she'd realized that mob violence might result.

Tex hadn't expected this trouble nor had he anticipated thinking about a girl when he was in the middle of it.

He grinned savagely, without humour, the expression being a mere quirk of the lips, at the realization that in the middle of a jam like this he was making excuses for the girl who had let him in for it – deliberately. Maybe she hadn't intended a lynching, maybe she'd thought it would be a matter of running him out of town and nothing else. What the heck did it matter to him what she'd thought or why she'd acted that way? It was likely that before long he wouldn't have any interest in girls, helpless ones or the other sort.

The seething cavalcade swept along, Tex bound to the saddle and pretty near jolted out of his senses when the rough section of the trail was reached. After a couple of miles they came to the crest of a rise and there, as Tex could see was a single, straight tree. A bough jutted out from the trunk, across the trail. It was about nine or ten feet from the ground – just about right for a lynching.

Desperately Tex strained at the cords round his wrists but it was no use.

'OK, get him off,' shouted Buck.

They brought Tex off the pony and let the beast go loose. By now the rest of the mob had come up and had formed a ring round the tree. There was a lot of shouting and excitement. Tex saw the faces in the moonlight. They didn't look like human faces. He recognized some, those he'd seen earlier at the hotel; at the back of the crowd he saw Pop Dwight, Linda's pal. He was quieter than the rest, but he was here all right and not making any attempt to interfere. Not that he could have done much anyway. The crowd was out of hand and after blood.

Buck jabbed Tex with his Colt.

'Get under the rope, mister,' he rasped.

There was a roar of approval from the mob. Tex wasn't given a chance to obey, however, for the huge Jeb jerked him forward and swung him to the appointed spot. Snake slipped the noose round his neck.

'OK, string him up,' ordered Buck.

Jeb reached up and grabbed the taut line of rope which ran from the trunk where it was fastened, to the end of the bough. It ran at an angle and Jeb grasped it about a quarter of the way along, where he could reach it. He exerted his weight, pulling down. It was a queer way of stringing up a guy, but Tex was in no condition to notice that.

The noose tightened round his neck and he was swung off his feet as Jeb's weight caused the rope to run over the bough.

The victim's feet left the ground, dangled, kicking, for his ankles had not been bound. There was a roaring in his ears as the blood pounded, a red mist formed in front of his eyes . . . he was choking.

And then at a signal from Buck, the rope was released by Jeb and Tex fell a couple of feet back to solid ground.

There was a roar from the mob, vaguely heard by Tex as he lay on the ground, his senses coming back. He had been suspended for only about thirty seconds, long enough to send him tottering to the very brink of unconsciousness but not long enough to push him over the edge.

He heard Buck Forbes yelling, and gradually the mob fell silent.

'OK, boys, that's enough of lynchin',' shouted Buck. 'We ain't stickin' out our necks for a no-good guy like this . . . there's a new Governor at Phoenix and we ain't takin' risks. But I guess he knows now what it feels like to be strung up. Now we'll turn him loose and I guess he won't come back for any more. If he does we'll string him up properly next time.'

There was confused noise from the mob, but Buck had his gun out covering them, and so had Jeb and Snake. Tex staggered to his feet realizing that it had been a frame-up, that there hadn't been any intention to lynch him, only to scare him off. It had been ingenious and in its way devilish. Tex reckoned, as his brain cleared, that probably the Parson had slipped the word to Buck and his boys what to do, otherwise Jeb and Snake wouldn't be playing in with Buck.

Even now it wasn't certain that a lynching wouldn't take place, because the nondescript mob outnumbered the Parson's guys. They might decide not to be disappointed in their expectation of a lynching.

It looked that way, because after a brief, stunned silence, somebody from the back let out a shout.

'That don't go down . . . string him up, boys, an' make a job of it this time.'

It needed only this spark to fire the gunpowder. The demand was taken up, a roar of approval arose and the mob, by now mostly dismounted, began to move forward dangerously. Again Tex strained at the cords round his wrists but it was useless; they held. He'd have given a lot to be free with a gun in his hand right now.

Buck tried to bring the mob to their senses, brought up his gun.

'Cut it out. . . .'

But it was no good, the boys were after blood and didn't much care if some of their own was spilled in the process. Pushed on from behind, the front ranks moved in.

And then a gun cracked out, but not from near the tree, not fired by Buck or the Parson's boys with him. The shot came from behind the mob. A man called out in pain . . . the mob halted, swung round. A second shot and a third cracked out. Two other men, at the back of the crowd, fell; and then there was pandemonium. Off the trail, behind the crowd, were clustered jagged rocks. The shots had come from these; the flashes of one or maybe two Colts pinpointed the direction.

The attack was utterly unexpected, the mob packed so close together that a miss was impossible. For a brief moment the cowhands stayed where they were, but then as two more shots rang out, each one hitting a man, the crowd broke. They forgot about Tex, forgot about the lynching they'd wanted. Even if there was only one guy attacking from behind the rocks he could achieve a heck of a lot of damage unless they got under cover.

They broke . . . and as they did so, as Buck, Jeb and Snake also made for cover, the trail being littered on both sides with rocks and outcrops, a figure materialized from the stunted bushes growing ten yards from the tree. Tex heard a slight sound and swung round. As he did so he saw the figure clearly within two yards of him, dressed in black, a black kerchief covering the face. In one hand was a gun, in the other something that gleamed silver under the moon – a knife.

'OK, take it easy,' muttered the guy, his voice muffled under the mask.

The knife was raised, slashed through the thick cords as though they were butter. They fell away and Tex's hands were free. A gun was thrust at him.

'Grab hold, mister, an' beat it,' said the newcomer.

Tex wasn't waiting to argue, wasn't waiting to work it out that this was the Kid . . . that much was obvious anyway. Tex took the Colt and vamoosed, making for the bushes. They didn't offer good cover, but beyond them lay broken ground and outcrops.

As he went firing broke out behind him, but not aimed at him. The mob hadn't got itself exactly organized yet, but they'd all made cover and now were loosing off at the rocks from behind which the first attack had been made.

Tex reached the bushes, flung himself down, the Colt comforting in his hand. Then he realized that the Kid had gone, vanished. He'd come like a ghost and now he'd disappeared like one. Unless Tex had known from the fact that he was now free with a gun in his hand that the guy had come in the first place, he could have doubted it.

There was a heck of a lot of shooting going on, ragged volleys all aimed at the rocks on the other side of the trail. But Tex realized that there was no return fire. He reckoned that whoever had launched the first attack had vamoosed. The Kid had operated with only one companion when holding up Jeb and Snake, or so it had seemed. It was likely therefore that his buddy had made the attack from behind the rocks, had made it alone, while the Kid waited his chance near the tree. Now the buddy had probably scrammed; if he could move anything like the Kid then he was well away by now and out of danger.

Tex had something to thank the Kid for, and his side-kick. They'd got him out of a jam that it hadn't seemed possible he could get out of. How they'd come to be around the place at the right moment he didn't know – maybe they'd followed the mob up the trail, maybe they'd been hanging about by accident. It didn't matter, and now wasn't the time to try and work it out. Tex had got to get away. Sure he had a gun now, but if the mob came to their senses and realized they were shooting at nothing they'd probably get after him. Tex wasn't waiting for that to happen.

He saw and heard a shadow moving away to his left; but it was a four-footed shadow. His beast had smelled him out. Tex was pretty well as glad to see the animal as he had been to feel a gun in his hand once more. He moved cautiously, keeping the scrub between him and the mob, still lying around under cover firing at the rocks. He came up to the pony, swung himself into the saddle and was away, aiming north, the only direction open to him though it wasn't the way he wanted to go. He'd been treated pretty rough, but Tex wasn't reckoning on leaving the Grant's River district. He'd come in response to an appeal by Sam Steel and he wasn't pulling out.

He wasn't pulling out – but he didn't aim to get grabbed again by the River crowd. On the whole he reckoned that the cowhands probably wouldn't try it on any more, not once they'd cooled off, which maybe was happening already but in any case would happen by morning if Tex knew anything about mob psychology. But there remained the Parson's set-up. They wouldn't pull out and they wouldn't cool off, not off the racket the Parson was working here in the Grant's River territory. That was a certainty. It was a certainty as well that the Parson himself was dangerous and so were his boys.

There was another reason why Tex wasn't going to put Grant's River behind him. He wasn't admitting as much even to himself, but it was a fact that if there had been no racket to investigate, no Dave Brand or Sam Steel to help, Tex Scarron would still have hung around. He'd heard a lot in his time about the influence a girl could exert over a guy; now he was finding out that the tales hadn't been exaggerated. He was finding that out but refused to admit it. Just the same it was a fact. He wanted to see more of Linda Forbes.

He had an eye and a feeling for country. And in this case he was helped by his boyhood memories of the territory. Landmarks he had forgotten until he saw them again came back to him when they loomed out of the landscape, lit by the moon now beginning to sink. He was riding north, towards the Black Hills, though he was off the trail he had followed earlier when riding to the River with the girl and the Parson's boys. There was no sound of pursuit; he reckoned he'd turn west after a bit, cross the trail on the River side of the pass and work his way back towards the settlement. He'd bypass it, though, and make for the Bar X, which lay west of Grant's River. It was mighty late by now, long past midnight and maybe the ranch would be sleeping. He couldn't help that and he reckoned Sam and Dave would be pleased enough to see him at any time.

Sure, they'd be pleased, or at all events Sam would be. Maybe Dave would have second thoughts when he found out why Tex had come, because according to Sam's letter old Dave wasn't the guy he had been. He was knuckling under, didn't want trouble. But there again Tex couldn't help it. Some guys had to be helped even against themselves.

He rode on. The hills loomed up ahead, a jagged line across the sky. Tex pulled in ready to turn west and cross the trail. As he did he heard something behind him, turned and caught a brief glimpse of a rider coming after him.

It was impossible to tell at that distance who it was, for the rider appeared only as a shadow. Tex was taking no risks. He wheeled his beast and made west for the trail, using a twisting, narrow track which wound between the outcrops. After another half-mile, with the trail itself not far ahead, he halted again. Sure, once more he could hear the faint sound of hoofs on loose stones. The guy was after him all right, it hadn't been chance that he was hanging around here.

Tex reckoned maybe he could lose him, but he didn't want to. He could attend to one hombre without trouble. He'd like to find out who it was and what he knew.

He pushed on, eyes scanning the territory for a spot to suit his purpose. After a bit he found one, on the other side of the trail. He had crossed the trail openly, without attempting to conceal his movements. The guy who was following him might as well be given a good lead to his route.

On the other side of the trail the track which he had been using continued, passing through a miniature defile. It was edged on either side by cliffs, which were nothing like so high as those of the hill pass, however. They rose only some thirty feet, could be reached easily enough, as Tex saw at a glance. He glimpsed the defile well ahead, pushed on hard, aiming to grab a lead long enough to enable him to lay his ambush.

He managed that all right. On one side of the track the cliff sloped down. Tex swung off his pony, led it off the track and tethered it out of sight. Then on foot he climbed the slope and so came to the top of the cliff. The position was ideal. He could cover the whole of the narrow defile beneath him.

The other guy hadn't come into sight yet but Tex could hear him on his way. The timing had been just right.

Tex had his gun out now, was crouched behind a boulder watching the eastern end of the defile. He'd glimpsed the guy a few moments earlier farther along the track. Any minute now he'd come into sight again.

He did, entered the defile and began to move along it. His eyes were on the surface of the trail. Just after he'd entered the defile he pulled up, foxed for the moment by the lack of prints, as Tex reckoned.

He wasn't foxed for much longer. Tex came upright, his gun steady on the guy.

'OK, stick 'em up,' he called, 'I've got you cold . . . don't reach for your rod.'

CHAPTER 6

It was Pop Dwight down there in the defile.

He located Tex quickly enough and his hands went up, but slowly

– and Pop didn't seem unduly worried.

'Hiya, Mister Scarron,' he called back. 'Guess you've pulled a fast one, but don't go gettin' trigger-happy, I ain't gunnin' for you.'

Tex wasn't arguing about that, wasn't yet ready to talk about why Pop had been on his trail.

'Pull out your guns and unload,' he called. 'An' don't try anythin' on.'

Pop didn't try anything on. He brought out his guns one after the other and unloaded them. When this was done Tex came down from the cliff. Pop's blue eyes surveyed him quietly. There was a small smile at his lips.

'What next, mister? You're bein' mighty particular.'

'That's right, I nearly handed in my checks tonight, remember? I ain't takin' no chances. Get off your horse.'

Pop Dwight climbed out of the saddle. He still didn't seem to be worried.

'Sure, I remember, I was there,' he said. 'I don't hold with lynchin' myself, but there wasn't a lot I could do, not against that bunch. I was glad when you made a break for it. How did you make it? Maybe you had some pals around the place?'

Tex wasn't answering these questions. The way he looked at it he was the guy who should be asking, Pop doing the answering. By now he was sure that nobody else was on the trail. They were alone up here among the foothills.

'What were you trailin' me for?' he asked. 'Reckon I don't go big for the tale you weren't gunnin' for me . . . you're the girl's buddy, ain't you?'

Pop's eyes, pretty shrewd eyes, Tex judged, sharpened. Tex was making sure of covering him but the guy didn't seem to be worrying about that. Tex might not have had a rod in his hand for all the notice Pop took of it.

'Sure . . . if you're talkin' about Linda.' And then, 'But I don't get why that makes you work out I was gunnin' for you.'

Tex twisted his lips.

'You don't? She got me into that trouble,' jerking his head towards the trail and the now distant Lone Point. 'Sure, she handed that out, deliberate,' he added.

Pop Dwight said nothing. Tex spoke again – he hadn't all night to spend fencing with words. His gun came up suggestively.

'Talk,' he rasped. 'You were trailin' me – what for?'

'OK, mister. I didn't see you make your break, but when the guys down there were beginnin' to work it out they were shootin' at nothin' I kinda moved around and then I picked up your trail. I followed along aimin' to get alongside and have a talk. It's like this, I once heard tell of a guy called Scarron who hung out in these parts when he was a boy. I heard this guy was pretty tough and had busted up a few rackets in his time . . . one in Colorado for instance, when he got Indian Bill an' put him away. When I heard you were called Scarron I reckoned you were the same guy.'

Tex stared at Pop. The newssheet owner had got his facts right so far as he'd gone. Tex had broken up quite a few rackets in his time, hiring himself out as a sort of private law enforcement officer. Two years back in Colorado he'd got the notorious Indian Bill, the gold bandit.

'OK, so I'm Scarron,' he said. 'What about it?'

Pop scratched his chin reflectively.

'I guess I worked out that bein' the guy who got Indian Bill you weren't a sharper,' he said after a pause. 'I worked out maybe the Parson's boys had been stackin' the deck, not you . . . or it could be you pulled a fast one on 'em knowin' they were crooks.'

He was still watching Tex closely and nodded to himself when he'd said his last piece.

'Sure, you'd lifted a packet off Spike, an' I guess nobody does that without pullin' a fast one. But it don't signify . . . knowin' who you were I worked out you were down in these parts maybe for a pretty good reason. Sam Steel was livin' here when you were a boy, they tell me, and Sam is in with Dave Brand at the Bar X these days.'

Tex was thinking fast. As had often happened in the past he'd got to use his experience and judgment of men. His instinct right now was to believe that Pop Dwight was on the level.

'What reason would I have for comin' here?' he asked.

The answer came without hesitation.

'The Parson's racket . . . that'd be good enough reason for a guy like you. You wouldn't have heard anythin' about what goes on in these parts, would you? Maybe from Sam at the Bar X? Yep, I reckon that's it, I reckoned so from the start . . . that'd explain why the Parson was mighty glad to have you run out o' town. I was aimin' to have a talk with you 'bout the Parson, that's why I followed along. You can put up your gun, mister, I ain't playin' in with the Parson, you can take that as hard.'

The two men stared at each other in silence, then Tex Scarron slowly put up his gun. He was willing to back his hunch that this guy was on the level – leastways until he had evidence that he wasn't. If he'd come gunning for him it didn't make sense that he'd have come alone, not a middle-aged guy like this well past his prime; and certainly not if he knew something about Tex Scarron's career, which undoubtedly he did.

'OK, we'll talk friendly,' he grunted. 'Maybe you've got somethin', maybe the Parson had a hunch why I'd come and wanted me run out o' town. But that don't explain why the girl wanted to get shot o' me. What you know about that?'

Pop Dwight shrugged his shoulders. There wasn't any accounting for women, he said. Linda was all right, he liked her. He reckoned she'd acted the way she thought was right, not knowing what Pop himself knew about Tex Scarron.

'But my guess is she didn't bank on any lynchin' nor on fake lynchin' they handed out,' he added. 'She don't come into this,' he continued, 'I reckon she don't know rightly what's goin' on, she's only been here a year. I reckon I can take it as hard you're here after Parson?'

Tex had been thinking how much he ought to reveal and now had come to a decision. As he saw it there wasn't much point in trying to bluff either Pop or the Parson and his set-up. Like Pop he thought probably the Parson had wanted him run out of town because he'd worked it out he was dangerous. When it was known that he was still in the district Dean would suspect even more strongly why he was staying in these parts. If Pop Dwight was bluffing and took word back to the Parson, or if he was indiscreet and opened his mouth too wide it wouldn't make a lot of difference. And anyway it might be an idea to let the Parson know the truth. That might push him into some unplanned and hurried move, with advantage to Tex. That had happened before. Coming out into the open often paid dividends.

And apart from any of this there was Tex's hunch that Pop was on the level. In that case he could be useful. More useful if he was let in on the facts.

'Sure, I'm here after the Parson,' replied Tex slowly. There were several points he wanted to discuss, including Linda Forbes and her activities, but they could wait for a bit. First things must come first. 'Yep, I'm after the Parson . . . I got word about his mutual protection racket. Seems like he's milkin' the territory. Dave ain't standin' up to it so well – he's my uncle, I got a family interest in this.'

Pop Dwight nodded. Then he spoke.

'It's 'bout time somebody busted this racket. I guess I've been thinkin' that for some time, but I ain't got what it takes any longer, I'm gettin' old, son. I ain't sayin' I'm proud o' what I've done, payin' out to the Parson every month because I was scared that otherwise he'd set his boys on to the *Gazette*, but there wasn't much I could do on my own.'

'Ain't there any other guys with guts?' asked Tex.

Pop Dwight shrugged his shoulders, but before he could reply there came an interruption. The silence of the night was shattered abruptly by the sound of a shot fired somewhere to the west, 'way in the distance. It was followed by another . . . and then there was silence.

Tex jerked round, listening. He estimated that the shots had come from at least a mile away, maybe more, for there was a wind from the west which would carry the sound quite a way. It seemed that he and Pop weren't the only guys up here among the outcrops. Events had sure moved fast since Tex had first set foot on Grant's River territory, and they were still moving.

His hand went to his gun-belt and came away with cartridges, which he thrust at Pop.

'Get your rods loaded,' he snapped. 'I reckon we'll get movin' – that way,' jerking his head towards the west. 'You reckon the Parson's boys might have come this way?'

'Maybe . . . not the mob, I should say they've got themselves back to the River by now, they ain't got guts enough to make a night of it lookin' for you, but it could be some o' the Parson's boys are hereabouts. Or maybe it's your buddies,' he added.

Tex didn't reply. The same thought had come to him that perhaps the Kid and the other guy who had helped him, supposing that there hadn't been more than one, were loosing off at something – or someone. But he wasn't talking. So far Pop Dwight didn't know who had helped him out of the jam at Lone Point. There was no time now to explain.

Tex made for his tethered pony and swung into the saddle. A few moments later he and Pop were riding hard along the defile making for the west. As they came to the end of the gorge another shot cracked out, enabling Tex to fix the direction more accurately.

Stretching away from the end of the defile was a wide sweep of broken ground unsuitable for grazing beeves, for here the hills were very close at hand, flinging up outcrops until the cow country farther south was reached. The moon was sinking pretty fast but it still provided some light; and in Arizona in summer the night was never very dark.

There was a view of the barren land stretching away to the west, broken ground scattered with massive boulders and with outcrops of the hills jutting up in grotesque formations. Tracks, most of them natural, left by water which in winter gushed down from the hills, wound between the outcrops. Far away in the distance there were more hills, higher than the Black Hills, for the range swept round in a giant semi-circle, enclosing some twenty square miles of barren ground, which farther south, well before the river was reached, became good grazing country.

The waning moon glimmered on the dark hills 'way ahead, and

on the outcrops nearer at hand; but the light was dim, deceptive, the area full of shadows. Tex reined in, realizing that without another lead it was an impossible task to hunt down whoever was indulging in gunplay. Maybe the gunplay didn't link up with the job that had brought him to the territory, maybe it didn't have any connection with the swiftly-moving events of the past hours, but Tex wanted to know about that for certain. Whichever way he looked at it this district of Grant's River didn't seem to be lacking in action.

He needed another lead right now, for though the last shot had given him the direction it hadn't pin-pointed the exact position. The hombres might be pretty well anywhere among the outcrops.

Pop Dwight pulled up alongside Tex. He could tell him something about this particular area, something Tex had forgotten. There was a minor trail which branched off the main trail south of the settlement, beyond the river. It doubled back, crossed the river at a ford and struck through the waste land, through a second pass in the Black Hills and so eventually rejoined the main trail not far from Indian Creek. Whoever was shooting might have come from Indian Creek, using the minor trail, or more likely had come from Grant's River. It could be that word had reached the Parson that the mob had struck unexpected trouble at Lone Point and he'd sent some of his boys by the minor, shorter trail to try and catch up with Tex – and those who had rescued him.

'Maybe,' grunted Tex. 'Keep your eyes skinned, Pop.'

There was no need, for when the next shot sounded, a matter of seconds after Tex had given his instruction, the stab of flame flashed out clearly about half a mile ahead. It was answered from a point to the north, nearer to the hills.

Tex had got what he needed now. There were either two guys shooting it out, one under cover behind an outcrop to the north of the narrow track which was a continuation of that which passed through the defile, the other south behind a cluster of rocks; or there were more than two. But at all events there was a gun battle being fought. Tex reckoned he'd got to find out what was going on and why.

There was more cover to the south than to the north. Tex decided to make in that direction, working round behind the rocks to get a sight of whoever was lying up there. It wouldn't be easy and there was always the possibility that Pop Dwight wasn't on the level. In that case he might grab an opportunity to pull a fast one while the reconnaissance was proceeding. But Tex had to take that chance. He couldn't do anything but have Pop along with him. To send him north or leave him by the defile would provide him with an even better opportunity to try something on – if he felt that way. Tex had got to trust him up to a point, reckoned that he could, but he wasn't going to trust him more than he had to. He wasn't leaving him on his own. Taking everything into consideration he was willing to back his judgment of the man but not too far.

'OK Pop, we'll get around behind that cover,' he said, pointing south. 'Leave your beast here.'

They dismounted and then taking advantage of all the cover they could find, began to move south-west, leaving the rocks where the unknown had chosen to hide up well to their right. There wasn't much difficulty at first, especially when a couple of shots sounded from the north, for these held the attention of whoever lay behind the rocks. Tex reckoned there wouldn't be much to spare for suspecting movement in the rear.

Tex made sure he kept Pop Dwight close to him and at least half a pace in front. And he wasn't aiming to get too near the hideout, not yet. Behind, to the south, there was a rise in the ground, some hundred yards behind the rocks. If he could reach that crest, maybe he could get a sight of the unknown guy or guys. After that he could work out what to do next.

They reached the ridge easily enough, crossing it three hundred yards from the cluster of rocks and thereafter being concealed by it. They moved along its other side and then turned up it. They came to the crest and could see movement behind the rocks which were now dead ahead of them.

It was a vague movement, but there were a couple of guys down there crouched under cover from the front but not from where Tex and Pop were stationed. That was as much as Tex could see.

'Guess we got to get nearer,' muttered Pop in his ear. 'Reckon we can make it.'

It looked like it, for thirty yards down the slope were other rocks offering concealment. Pop Dwight could move silently enough, as Tex by now knew. He'd have preferred to move down the slope alone, leaving Pop on the ridge, but he didn't fancy having anyone but a proved buddy in his rear with a gun. He'd got to get nearer to the hideout. He wanted to know who was gunning down there; and in any case even if he dispensed with this project and decided to break up the shooting straight away, in this light the range was too long from the crest for effective action.

'OK, get down to the rocks,' replied Tex, 'and don't go makin' a noise.'

They made down the slope, Pop in front. Tex noted, as he'd done already, that the guy knew how to move. He wasn't as young as he had been, he'd been right in what he'd said about that, but he wasn't past it yet. And judging by the way he handled his gun he knew how to use it.

Maybe he reckoned he wasn't up to taking a stand against the Parson, but it could be he'd pulled a fast one over that. The thought came to Tex as he watched him move down the slope. It wasn't that Tex yet doubted his judgment that Pop was on the level, he still reckoned he was. But one small portion of his mind told him that the possibility that he wasn't must be kept in view.

Tex followed after and came to the good cover of the rock. Now a better view could be had of the two guys at the bottom of the slope. One of them half turned his head and then Tex knew who it was. The hombre was masked; and he was dressed in black. This was the Kid again, arrived here by some other route.

Pop saw the mask at the same instant. He let fall an exclamation and brought up his gun. The Kid was a sitting target, unaware that he was menaced from the rear.

As Pop brought up his gun Tex grabbed his wrist. The Kid was a bandit all right, no doubt about that, he'd provided plenty of proof, but he'd got Tex out of a bad jam. Tex wasn't having the guy bumped off, not in cold blood from the rear.

He grabbed Pop's wrist and the gun went off simultaneously. The bullet did no damage but ricocheted off the ground a few yards in front of Pop as the Colt was jerked down. It did no damage but the shot was enough to warn the Kid and his companion. They swung round, there were a couple of rapid shots, with Tex and Pop ducking back under cover, and then the guys were under cover themselves, round behind the end of the line of rocks they were using.

'Heck,' muttered Pop Dwight, 'what you reckon. . . ?'

He broke off as there came the noise of hoofs on loose stones. The Kid and his buddy must have had their beasts tethered out of sight behind the rocks. Now they were away.

Pop got to his feet, his gun up again. He loosed off a couple of shots but it was no good. The Kid was away and with him the other, mere vague shadows in the waning light, striking west.

There was no possibility of pursuing, for Tex and Pop had left their ponies 'way back near the end of the defile. Pop swung round on Tex.

'Hey, what's the idea? What you want to go interferin' for? I had that bird taped . . . it was the Kid.' He broke off as a thought came to him. 'Sure, you knew that, I guess. Maybe I've made a mistake, Scarron, maybe you ain't on the level . . . are you workin' in with the Kid?'

'You got it all wrong, Pop. I ain't in with the Kid, but he was the guy who loosed me up at Lone Point and I reckoned I owed him somethin' for that. But the score's even now. I won't be stallin' any more with the Kid.'

Pop Dwight stared at Tex. Then gradually he relaxed.

'OK, Scarron I'll take your word for it,' he muttered. 'It looked kinda funny, but . . . aw, skip it. Guess we'd better get back to the track.'

They scrammed for the ponies. There was at least one other guy, and maybe more, hiding up to the north, within range, but the Kid and his buddy must have been seen high-tailing and it was unlikely that whoever had been gunning was still around. In any event Tex would feel happier mounted.

They reached the tethered ponies and remounted. Hardly had they done so when Pop grabbed Tex by the arm.

'Somebody comin',' he grunted.

Within seconds a mounted figure came vaguely into sight, riding from north to south, crossing the track which Tex and Pop had now rejoined. Whoever it was, and to Tex it was only an unidentifiable figure, crossed the track about halfway between the end of the defile and the hideout where the Kid had been lying up. The figure passed swiftly from view, aiming due south towards the distant settlement.

'Doc Black,' muttered Pop, 'I guess you can't miss the way he rides, got caught up in mill rollers 'way back and that crippled his shoulder.'

As he spoke he jerked at the reins of his pony, aiming to go after the solitary rider, but he didn't get any farther. A voice spoke from behind.

'Get your hands up an' make it quick.'

Then, as Tex and Pop swung round, to find themselves covered by a guy who on foot had slid out from behind cover, there came a vivid oath and the menacing gun was lowered.

It was Sam Steel who had pulled a fast one on Tex, Sam Steel who now gazed at him like he was seeing a ghost.

CHAPTER 7

Dave Brand, owner of the Bar X, a man well over sixty and looking even older, stared across the room at Tex. His grey face was lightened by an expression in his eyes which Sam Steel for one hadn't seen there for a long time. There was a new strength about Dave right now, the dawning of what Sam thought might be a new resolution.

It was now the early hours of the morning, though dawn had not yet broken. Sam Steel had brought Tex and Pop Dwight to the Bar X after meeting up with them in the foothills. Now, with Dave Brand, they were in the shabby but spacious living-room of the ranch, which like most others in the district gave on to a verandah running the length of the building.

Dave had been in bed asleep when the party arrived, but he'd got up quickly enough when he heard that Tex had come. Pretty well the first thing he said surprised the newcomer.

'You got my letter, Tex? Sure . . . I reckoned I could rely on you. We've heard somethin' of what you've done in other parts. I judged you'd come along here if you could.'

Tex had received no letter from his uncle, only from Sam; but it seemed Dave had written, and along the same lines as Sam.

'Heck, Dave, I didn't know,' muttered the corpulent Sam, whose round, rosy face wasn't very different from what it had been as a boy, but which was a mask for a pretty good standard of efficiency. 'I aimed to get Tex along, but . . . I thought you were still foldin' up and takin' what the Parson handed out,' he added.

It didn't look like it was that way at all, though. Now Tex was watching Dave closely, marking the changes the years had wrought in face and figure. He reckoned that if he'd been in Sam's place he'd have thought the same – that Dave had folded up. His shoulders were hunched, his face lined, far more than it should have been merely as a result of passing years. It was difficult to define, to say just why he was sure that Dave Brand wasn't the man he'd known in the old days, but Tex was dead certain as he watched him standing there in the living-room. Something had gone out of Dave. He'd folded up, that was as good a description as any.

Folded up . . . but just the same a spark of the old Dave seemed to have been struck after all. He had written to Tex, hoping his letter would reach him, asking him to come down to the Bar X, outlining some of the troubles which were besetting the ranch – and others in the district. This Tex now knew for Dave had explained. It seemed he hadn't known that Sam also had written.

'OK, it don't signify,' said Tex now, breaking the silence. 'I didn't get your letter, Dave, I've been movin' around, but I got Sam's and vamoosed along here.'

Dave broke in, scraping his hand over his unshaven jaw. He knew nothing of events, even less than Sam Steel.

'What you mean, Tex? Ain't you just come?'

'I've been around a few hours. I'll give you the dope, but I reckon first I could do with hearin' your tale, and Sam's. He's told me a bit but not everythin'. And there's Pop here. He's got a bit to say. After that we can get down to business . . . if you ain't too tired, Dave?'

Again his eyes flickered over the face and figure of this man who when he had last seen him, some years before, had been straight and upright, tough, efficient and virile. There was a great change now. Dave Brand was old, old not only in body but in spirit. To Sam Steel, his friend and foreman, he wasn't looking so bad as he had done for the last two or three years, a flicker of the old Dave had come to life since Tex had arrived; but to Tex he looked in a bad way. Tex felt pity for Dave, remembering as he did the old days, when the Bar X had been such a prosperous outfit. He had only to glance round this living-room to realize how things had changed. In Mrs Brand's time the room had been spotless and well-furnished. Now it was shabby, untidy and dirty. And during the ride from the foothills, across Bar X property, Tex had used his eyes. He'd noted the fences in need of repair, the general air of dilapidation.

On one point, however, he had been agreeably surprised. According to Sam's letter Dave had lost all will to fight, even will to live. Tex had expected no great welcome when Dave found out why he had come. Instead of that Dave wanted him, had sent for him. That was something. It was easier to help a guy who wanted to be helped.

'I ain't tired,' muttered Dave, in answer to the last question. Then he looked across at Pop Dwight, who hadn't said very much since riding in. 'I don't get what Pop's got to do with this.'

'We'll get around to that later,' replied Tex. 'How 'bout you talkin' first, Dave? Give me all you've got about the trouble hereabouts an' then I'll do some talkin'. I got a few questions to ask . . . guess you know the Lazy Y outfit and the Forbes, Buck and the girl called Linda?'

It was Sam who answered. Sure they knew the Lazy Y, but why was Tex interested in the dame?

'She's the only skirt I ever knew who could look after herself,' he added, 'but I don't get. . . .'

'Leave it, Sam, I'll explain later. Dave, give me your slant.'

When Sam had been so unexpectedly encountered in the foothills not much explanation had been given either by Sam or Tex. The latter knew, briefly, why Sam had been hanging around there, knew that he'd approached the gun battle from the north but had been too late to take any sort of part in it. He got there just after the Kid and his companion had been surprised by Tex and Pop. He'd seen some other guys, but they'd broken up and cleared by the time Sam had encountered Tex. Tex had decided to get to the Bar X without further delay and have a talk with Dave.

Dave sat down heavily in a shabby chair and Pop Dwight followed suit, making use of the liquor Dave had brought out from a cupboard. Tex remembered that even as a boy Sam had always liked looking after people. Now he hovered around Dave anxiously, producing a bottle of medicine before Dave started to talk and making him take a dose.

'You know what Doc Black said,' he muttered, 'your heart ain't what it was, Dave. You swallow some o' this.'

Tex felt the old affection for Sam. He'd always been a good guy had Sam, and he was the same way now. It didn't take much working out that during the past years he'd kept the Bar X going and tended the old man as well, like he was his son. A good guy Sam, and tough as well, when it was necessary. Leastways, he'd been tough in the past and Tex reckoned he hadn't changed.

'OK, this is the set-up,' said Dave, when he had swallowed the draught Sam poured out for him. But then he hesitated, looking across at Pop Dwight . . . and the expression in his eyes gave Tex the clue to his thoughts.

'It's OK, Dave, Pop is workin' with me. That right, Pop?'

'Sure, it's like I told you, it's 'bout time somebody with guts broke the Parson. That's plain enough, ain't it, Brand? You ain't got anythin' to worry about; I don't aim to go back to the River blabbin'.'

By now Tex had decided that Pop Dwight was on the level, definitely on the level. If he'd wanted to pull a fast one he could have done that without a lot of difficulty during the manoeuvres in the foothills, or at least made some attempt. Pop Dwight was OK and might prove pretty useful.

'You carry on, Dave,' said Tex, 'I want to get the set-up nice and tidy in my mind.'

So Dave talked, aided by Sam and Pop from time to time. Tex Scarron listened without interruption while the story was told. Basically it wasn't much different from the outline Sam had given him in his letter. The Parson had busted in on the Grant's River settlement and after a bit had started this mutual protection racket.

Tex listened to the yarn, which was embellished with more details than Sam had given him in his laboriously written letter. He heard how the Parson, having brought in Jeb and the guy Snake, plus a whole lot of other tough guys, had proved that protection was needed – by the simple expedient of burning down ranches, rustling cattle and committing at least one murder. Nothing could be proved and the Parson's tale was that bandits lying up in the hills had been responsible for these crimes. Nothing could be proved, but it was a certainty that the Parson's bunch, acting under his orders, had committed the crimes.

'Sure,' muttered Pop Dwight, 'an' the sheriff's been bought. That made it easier for the Parson.'

Tex grunted, remembering Poston and his attitude down at the hotel. The racket wasn't a new one, not in the cities; but this was the first time Tex had run across it elsewhere. Not that there was any reason why it shouldn't be worked in cow-country, quite a few reasons why it should pay better dividends. In the cities hoodlums had organized forces of law and order to combat as well as any resistance from their victims. Out here there was more scope and fewer obstacles.

Tex could understand that given sufficient tough guys who wouldn't stop at murder, given that the sheriff was bought, it would be a walk-over. Each ranch had its quota of cowhands, but the ranches were widely scattered and after generations there was a tradition of isolation. The district as a whole kept itself to itself; so did each individual ranch. There was no cohesion, with the result that the thugs could deal with each ranch separately.

'That's the way it's been,' stated Sam. 'At first nobody was fallin' for the Parson's racket, but by the time he'd operated a bit they were glad to. They pay him his dough every month and so long as they do that they're in the clear. But when some guy takes a stand and don't pay, things happen.'

Pop Dwight shifted uneasily in his chair.

'That's right, but I guess it's been our own fault. That don't sound so good comin' from me, maybe . . . I told you, Scarron, I ain't proud o' the way I've folded up. But it's a fact, I guess. We ought to have made a stand.'

Sam grunted, pouring himself some spirit.

'That's OK as talk, but it ain't no good one guy takin' a stand. Werner up at the Block Diamond, he's been runnin' a feud with the Tumblin' T for twenty years, and Josh Malloney up at Indian Range, he ain't talkin' to Werner nor anyone else. I tell you it just ain't possible to get these guys together.'

Tex wasn't surprised at this. It was pretty well known that the Grant's River territory was torn with feuds. There was sometimes gunning and always trouble of some sort. The Parson must have known this after he'd been at the River for a bit and worked it out that the area was ideal for his purpose.

It wasn't long before Tex had a good overall picture of the set-up. It was just about what he'd reckoned. By now the Parson, taking in his monthly dues regular, was sitting very pretty, a big man at the River, owning the Double K, the hotel, the gambling joint and other concerns, all bought with the profits from the original racket.

'OK Pop, you got anythin' to add?' Tex asked.

'Not much, I reckon. I've been payin' my dues same as the rest, otherwise the old Gazette would go. At the beginning I tried to stick out but some o' my plant was wrecked, by way of a warnin' and after that I played ball. But I'm ready to work in with you now. I ain't got no people, no wife an' no kids. I reckon I can afford to take a risk.' He paused and then heaved himself from his chair. 'And I guess you're the guy who maybe can break the Parson,' he added.

Sam Steel took him up, his chubby face set.

'That goes for me, too, Tex. Some o' what you been doin' up north got back here, you know the way it is. I reckoned you were the guy to give us a break. Maybe you can get some o' these other hombres to play in.' He looked sidelong at Dave and then added, 'Looks like Dave aims to play in. I didn't reckon on that, I worked it out we'd have to talk him round, but it looks like I was wrong.'

Dave Brand came clean then.

'I ain't been much good not since Mary died,' he said, his voice brittle. 'I let the place go down, been drinkin' too much . . . Sam could tell you. I folded up when the Parson tried it on. But I got around to thinkin' Mary wouldn't have liked that an' then I thought o' you, Tex. But that ain't all. I didn' go down to the River today to pay the Parson, an' I ain't goin'. If he wants his dough he'll have to come up here for it. I can still hold a gun and Sam can hit a haystack. I reckon some o' the boys will lend a hand. I reckoned that maybe if I stuck out that'd kinda encourage some o' the others. It's all we need . . . if we can get some o' them to stand in together we can finish the Parson and his bunch.'

There was silence in the room for a little. There was a spark of the old Dave Brand left all right, no doubt about that. He'd aimed to stand out against the Parson even before he'd known that Tex was coming. It took some guts, there wasn't any doubt about that, either. Tex had received proof that the Parson's bunch were ruthless. He knew now that at the Double K, the hotel and the other concerns owned by the Parson, there were well over a hundred tough guys, all employed by the Parson and under his orders. If they were set on to the Bar X there wouldn't be much left of the ranch by the time they'd finished. Maybe Dave's example would rally the other ranchers and make them forget their private quarrels, but maybe not. It might have the opposite effect. The example of the Bar X might well scare them into paying up for ever without asking for trouble.

Sam and Pop were evidently thinking along the same lines, though they didn't say anything. It was Tex who broke the silence which followed on Dave's statement.

'We'll talk about that later,' he said. 'Sam, I reckon I know you had word I'd been run out o' the River and the mob was after me, which was why you were ridin' through the foothills, but I guess you'd better give us all the dope about what you saw up there.'

Sam nodded briefly, going on to amplify the very brief explanation he'd already given Tex and Pop.

'Sure – one o' the boys came back from the River and let out there was a guy grabbed stackin' a poker deck down at the hotel. When he told me what this guy looked like I knew it was you, Tex, so I took out my beast and went to have a look-see. The guy told me the mob had taken you up the Black Hills trail.'

Sam had ridden well north and he'd heard shots just like Tex and Pop had heard them. He'd investigated and got a sight of four of the Parson's boys lying up exchanging shots with other guys south of the track near the defile. He hadn't known then what had happened to Tex, nor who the *hombres* were south of the track. But he recognized the Parson's boys.

After that he'd ridden towards the defile and there had come across Tex and Pop Dwight.

'I guess that's about all,' he said.

'Did you see Doc Black?' asked Tex. 'Maybe he was with the Parson's bunch?'

Sam shook his head. He hadn't sighted Black . . . he hadn't been one of the four hoodlums he'd seen a bit earlier.

'Heck, the Doc's OK,' he muttered. 'He's a good guy, he ain't workin' in with the Parson.'

'Maybe he ain't, but he was hangin' around,' said Pop. 'There ain't no mistakin' the way he rides, not with that shoulder o' his.'

Tex took over. It was time for him to tell his tale.

He recounted exactly what had happened to him after he left Indian Creek, starting with his meeting with Linda Forbes and ending with the encounter with Sam Steel by the defile. Tex was a better hand at talking than any of the others and he gave them the story lucidly, not leaving out anything of importance.

'I guess that's the lot,' he ended. He glanced at Pop and added, 'Now I reckon you know why I'm interested in the girl. Maybe she's a sucker and reckons the Parson is on the level. Maybe she did reckon I was a hoodlum and laid for me not knowin' who I was . . . and maybe like you said, Pop, she acted the way she thought was right when she had me run out o' town . . . but maybe none o' that is true.'

Sam Steel's round face puckered.

'She ain't no sucker,' he stated, 'you can take that as hard, Tex. She's a dame who knows what she's doin'. That's more'n you can say about Buck. The Parson's mob have been milkin' him, he's a sucker but he don't know it, thinks he's a mighty smart guy.'

Tex rolled a cigarette, lit it before replying. Sam knew that Buck Forbes was being milked, but apparently Linda didn't.

'Buck pays his dues?' asked Tex, when he'd lit the cigarette.

'I guess so,' was Sam's reply, 'but that ain't all he pays . . . I reckon he's been milked more than that.'

Pop Dwight was looking upset. He was fond of Linda, knew her pretty well, but it was only now, as he explained, that he'd got around to thinking that maybe it was mighty queer that she was friendly with the Parson and at least some of his boys.

'Leastways, maybe not exactly friendly,' he added, 'but she's always pleasant to 'em. I reckoned she was just a nice kid who didn't know what the Parson was. She's only been at the Lazy Y a year, like I told you. I thought she'd fallen for the tale that the Parson was doin' the River a good turn keepin' his mob to hold off bandits. But now I guess . . . I guess you're right, she ain't a sucker an' that means she wouldn't fall for the Parson's tale. You got me worried, Scarron.'

Tex didn't give anything away – not about the fact that he was worried, too. He didn't even admit as much to himself. Linda Forbes was a girl he'd met for the first time only a matter of hours before. She didn't mean anything to him, so he told himself.

'We don't know enough to work out anythin' definite,' he said, 'but we got to keep her in mind, she's been actin' queer. She ain't the only one at that. There's this Doc Black you say ain't in with the Parson, but he was up in the hills a while back and vamoosed pretty slick after the shootin'. And there's the Kid. I reckon the Parson got word I'd got clear. Maybe he sent some of his boys up the other trail to get me if they could, there was just about time, I got delayed talkin' to Pop. I guess they ran into the Kid instead. He got away OK I should say.'

This was likely enough, for Tex and Pop hadn't sighted the Parson's boys after the Kid, which they would have done if the bunch had got on the trail slickly. The Kid could be taken as being still at large.

Sam grinned, but without humour.

'I reckon the Parson ain't so pleased . . . you say the Kid lifted five hundred dollars off Jeb and Snake. That'd be the dough they got from Hackamore for dues. No, sir, I reckon the Parson don't take kindly to any other guy rustlin' in on his territory.'

Tex was inclined to agree, but at the moment he wasn't interested in the Kid or his buddy. If he stayed on in the district it might be that it would give the Parson something to think about and something to do, diverting his attention. That would be an advantage to Tex, if it happened; but at that point in the affair Tex reckoned that the Kid was only a side-line, whose impingement on the Parson case couldn't be more than incidental. He was wrong there but couldn't know it, not yet.

Dave Brand also brushed aside the subject of the Kid. He came back to something else, mentioned earlier.

'I ain't payin' the Parson,' he stated flatly. 'You don't reckon I ought to, Tex?'

Tex crossed to the glass door that gave on to the verandah. The dawn had broken by now and the corral and the home grazing-grounds showed starkly under the cold light. For a few moments he stood there staring out, before he turned back to Dave.

'I reckon I got ideas about that,' he said. 'You give me the low-down how much you're supposed to pay and how you get it to the Parson.'

Dave gave him what he wanted and Tex listened silently. When the old man had finished he nodded.

'OK, I'll tell you what we'll do, Dave.'

He talked for quite a bit, the others giving him their attention. It wasn't until the sun was up that Tex went to bed and Pop Dwight rode back to Grant's River.

CHAPTER 8

It was the next evening that Tex Scarron rode towards Grant's River. He was due to meet up with Pop Dwight pretty soon, but right now he was alone.

He had spent the day at the Bar X. He had arrived at the ranch so late on the previous night that nobody except old man Brand, Sam and Pop knew that he had come. Dave had put it around the next day that he had been awakened by Sam and Pop, making no mention of Tex. The latter had lain up during the day in the spare room, food being brought to him by Dave himself, when the cook, Martha, who looked after him and Sam, wasn't around. Nobody else lived in the ranch-house, the cowhands bunking in the log outbuilding nearby.

Tex couldn't manage to hide up for longer than the one day and in fact didn't want to. All he needed to ensure was that he got some rest undisturbed and that the Parson was kept in the dark regarding his whereabouts. Tex didn't want trouble until he was ready for it; and he didn't want the Parson bringing his boys up to the Bar X after him – or Dave Brand. He reckoned he'd made out all right. During the day, according to Dave and Sam, nobody had approached the Bar X.

Now Tex was ready to play his own hand. He'd summed up the position on the previous night and had found no reason since to change his mind about his conclusions. The Parson was working a very pretty little racket here. It had got to be broken, but Tex was against any rushing. He knew enough to realize that even if in the end it should prove possible to bring the ranchers of the district together and call a halt to the Parson's operations, this would take time. There were feuds between the ranches and apart from this consideration there was the fact that the ranchers were self-sufficient guys who had a reputation for not taking kindly to strangers. The odds against Tex being able to bring them together were long. As for Dave making a stand now and hoping that this would set an example which would be followed, Tex didn't go big for that. That had been tried, apparently, at the beginning and it hadn't worked.

Tex wasn't having Dave made a victim of the Parson's bunch and maybe losing the Bar X as a result. He'd talked the old man out of his fool idea. Dave and Sam had called him in and he was taking over. Dave had agreed. During the morning Sam had ridden down to the township and had paid over to the Parson the dues, saying that Dave was unwell and couldn't come himself. Tex reckoned that this would keep the Parson quiet for a bit, so long as he didn't know that the guy he'd had trouble with on the previous night was lying up at the ranch.

Time had thus been bought. Tex hoped to buy a bit more. He didn't see much chance of breaking the Parson himself, even with the assistance of Dave Brand and the Bar X cowhands. It wasn't by any means certain that the latter would play in and be prepared to run risks on Dave's behalf. It wasn't their dough that was being levied. A few might be willing to play in but not enough, Tex judged, to put the Parson out of business. The same would apply to the rest of the ranches.

There remained the possibility of getting the Parson through the forces of law and order. Tex had worked with the law before, knew that though some guys and some Governors were corrupt, a whole lot weren't. This new guy York was reported to be a go-getter. Tex reckoned he'd got to come in on this affair, but first more must be learned if possible. Hearsay and reported stuff wasn't enough. Tex wanted something more concrete before he tried tackling the Governor.

He'd left Dave and Sam at the Bar X, and was to rendezvous with Pop this side of the River. Pop had guaranteed to keep his mouth shut during the day about what had happened between him and Tex in the hills and about the talk at the Bar X. He'd also agreed to keep his eyes and ears open at the settlement, reporting to Tex when he met him.

Tex came to the rendezvous, a grotesque, steeple-shaped rock a hundred yards off the trail, a minor one which led from the Bar X to Grant's River. He made sure the trail was deserted and then turned off, making for the rock. It was not yet dark but dusk had crept up over the hills and the grazing-grounds. Tex neither saw nor heard Pop Dwight, came to the rock and reined in. He swung from the saddle, making sure his guns were loose in the sheaths.

Then, unheralded by any sound, Pop Dwight materialized from the shadows.

'OK, Scarron, there ain't nobody around,' grunted Pop. 'How you make out?'

'No interference, I got some shut-eye and I reckon I can tackle the Parson now. You got anythin' for me?'

Pop had something. Tex listened to what he had to say and knew that his hunch that Pop would be useful was working out.

The newssheet owner gave him the general background first. The mob who had run Tex out of town on the previous night had cooled off by morning, and Pop reported, after moving around among some of them during the day, that the first fine careless rapture was over and they were no longer anxious to grab Tex and lynch him. Tex wasn't surprised, it usually worked out that way. Once the effects of liquor had worn off and the guys were on their own, no longer influenced by a mob of companions, they pretty well always had second thoughts. The mob had been composed of cowhands; there had been no ranchers amongst them, except Buck Forbes.

Getting more specific, Pop talked about the Parson and his reactions.

'He sent some of his boys up into the foothills to try an' get you,' he grunted, 'I heard some of 'em talkin'. The Parson's mad they didn't catch up with you and now he knows the Kid and his buddy were hangin' around. He don't know for sure the Kid got you away, but he's worked it out that's what happened. He ain't so happy with you an' the Kid around.'

'He got any idea I've been up at the Bar X?' asked Tex.

'Nope, I don't reckon so. I saw Sam come in with the dough, like we arranged last night. Sam didn't see me an' neither did the Parson. I reckon the dollars'll keep him happy for a bit.' He paused and then added, 'I had a talk with Doc Black.'

'What did the Doc have to say?' he asked.

'Well, I reckon he went out o' his way to make out he was at home all last night,' drawled Pop slowly. 'I kinda chatted casual an' he took his chance – I reckon it was that way. There's a dame up in the hills expectin' a kid, I asked him if it had come yet an' he says no, he'd thought maybe he'd be called out last night but he wasn't, he got to bed early and stayed there. That don't link up with what we saw in the hills.'

It didn't, provided that Pop hadn't made a mistake and that it had been Doc Black riding near the defile. Tex had to rely on Pop for the identification.

'That's OK, it was the Doc for sure,' was the reply to this query. 'I tell you there ain't no mistakin' the guy, not with that shoulder o' his. He was ridin', an' I reckon with the Parson's boys.'

Tex was silent, chewing this over. Taking it that Pop was right and the Doc had been up in the hills, Tex couldn't work out what this particular set-up was. There didn't seem any reason why guys playing in with the Parson should fake they weren't. The Parson and his bunch were sitting pretty, must reckon they were in the clear, with no proof that the mutual protection racket was anything more than an on the level scheme to protect ranchers in the district. If the Doc was in with the Parson, why bluff? The hoodlums had been gunning against the Kid, and there wasn't any crime about that.

Tex couldn't work it out, but then at the time he didn't know anything about the fifty per cent cut of profits lying in the Parson's safe in a steel box.

'What about Buck Forbes . . . and the girl?' he asked. 'You seen either of 'em today?'

Pop shook his head. Buck hadn't shown up at the River during the day and according to what Pop had heard he had been out ranging Lazy Y property. As for Linda, she'd been out too, but not with her cousin.

'A guy told me he'd seen her up near the hills,' he said slowly. 'She gets around, like she was a man.' He paused and then added, 'You still reckon she's off the level?'

Tex chewed at his unlighted cigarette. He'd been thinking quite a bit about Linda Forbes during the day, but hadn't got anywhere with his thoughts. He had a hunch, which he didn't like, that she was mixed up in this Parson business.

'OK, Pop, you'd better get up to the Bar X an' wait for me there. I'll be back and maybe I'll know more then.'

Pop Dwight looked uneasy.

'You aim to take this on by yourself?' he asked. 'I reckon you'll be runnin' a risk.'

Tex touched the butt of one of his Colts. He was used to risks – and it was necessary to take this on without assistance.

'I'll make out, Pop. You get up to the Bar X and hang around. Sam an' Dave are there. Maybe you'd better go careful, don't let nobody see you.'

Pop gave in and presently Tex was riding towards the River, once more alone. He'd got away from the ranch without anyone seeing him and he judged that Pop ought to manage to arrive the same way. Sam and Dave were expecting him.

Tex rode on, aiming for Grant's River but not following the trail very long. Before the junction with the Black Hills trail, which became Main Street, he turned off, cutting across open country so as to approach the settlement from the flank. This way he could reach Main Street and the hotel without being seen. He'd deliberately waited until nightfall. He didn't want any trouble before he got to the hotel.

He left Bar X grazing ground and came to the edge of the tract of waste ground lying between him and the settlement. The place was still some distance but the lights were lit and he could see them twinkling ahead. The hotel was easily identified, not only by its bulk but by the bright flashes of naphtha light. Tex knew that barring accidents the Parson would be there, it being his habit to use the hotel as his headquarters. The Double K ranch was more of a blind than anything else and a place for his boys to lie up.

He reined in on the edge of the waste land, working out his best route to the rear of the hotel. Then, for a brief moment, he caught a glimpse of a rider 'way ahead but making roughly towards him. Some guy was leaving Grant's River by the same route he himself had decided to adopt.

Tex went under cover and waited. The rider came into sight again between two mounds of debris, came closer. But it wasn't a guy, it was a girl . . . it was Linda Forbes again. There wasn't any mistaking her even at that distance and in that light.

Tex made no movement but watched her. She was riding slowly and he thought carefully. Once she stopped and peered behind her at the lights of Grant's River. Tex, well out of sight, crouched under cover watching. She was a good-looking girl, all right. What else was she? Tex didn't know.

After a bit she moved on, passing within fifty yards of Tex but not seeing him. She disappeared in the direction of the Bar X trail. Tex wondered whether she was making for the ranch, but then dismissed the thought. If she was, Sam and Dave could look after her. He himself had other business to attend to.

When the noise of her progress had faded he moved on himself, cautiously crossing the waste ground and so coming to the rear of the hotel. By now the saloon should be pretty full. Tex reckoned he knew how to empty the place pretty quick, which was what he needed to do.

From Sam and Dave he'd learned enough about the lie of the land to serve his purpose, and about certain other matters, including the fact that the Parson used the hotel as his headquarters. Tex wanted a look at his private office, and maybe inside the safe he kept there.

He tethered his pony under cover fifty yards behind the hotel. Nobody was about, all was quiet. Then, avoiding the hotel for the time being, he moved on foot parallel with Main Street, passing behind the gambling joint owned by the Parson and so came to the other drinking saloon farther down the street and on the same side as the hotel.

It was a wooden building like the rest of Grant's River, the wood dry after the scorching sun of summer. Stacked behind the building were a dozen drums containing, as Tex had discovered, paraffin oil for lighting. There wouldn't be much difficulty in emptying the hotel. When the Parson knew what had happened at his other saloon he'd be out and on the spot quick enough and so would everyone else in the hotel.

Tex made sure there was nobody around and then rolled one of the drums to the rear wall of the saloon. The moon was higher now, the light stronger, but the building threw a deep shadow. Tex could hear plenty of noise coming from the saloon and there was life along Main Street, as he could see, for between the buildings were narrow alleys leading from the street to the waste ground. But the latter was deserted, with neither sound nor movement.

Tex wrenched off the cap of the drum, tipped it and let the oil flow out over the wooden wall. Then he brought out a length of cloth, twisted it, dipped it in the oil and laid it as a fuse to the drum.

He lit the fuse and scrammed swiftly back towards the hotel. When it reached the barrel there was a roar as the oil on the woodwork caught, and an explosion as the half-empty drum was fired. Instantly great tongues of smoky, red flame shot up, licking up the wooden wall.

Tex stayed where he was, in the deep shadow more than two hundred yards from the drinking saloon. He reckoned another few minutes would be enough to spread the alarm all over the settlement.

He was about right. There came the noise of confused shouting and then Tex saw shadowy figures come into view running hither and thither and apparently with not much idea of what to do about the fire, which had now taken devastating hold on the wooden building.

Then there came more shouting, this time from the hotel. Across the Main Street end of the alley Tex saw guys running down the street from the hotel towards the saloon. He heard heavy footsteps on the wooden verandah fronting Main Street. The hotel was emptying as he'd reckoned it would.

A few minutes later he judged that the hotel was empty. He'd seen the Parson himself crossing the mouth of the alley, along with Jeb and Snake and a whole lot of other boys. Some must have been cowhands who had been drinking at the bar, but it was a certainty the Parson had taken all his own boys with him. He wouldn't be exactly anxious to have his other joint go up in flames.

Tex slid along the alley, came to a window which he knew belonged to the room where he'd been grabbed on the previous night. He passed it and there was another window. He'd not been inside the Parson's office, but he knew where it was situated in relation to the other room. This window would give him entrance.

He didn't have any difficulty with the catch and swung himself over the sill into the room. The flames from the burning saloon farther down the street were now lighting up the sky. Great gouts of black smoke were drifting across Main Street, intershot with lurid fire. Tex had caught a glimpse of a mass of men crowded round the saloon, stretching across the street. Nobody could have been trapped inside the building, for it consisted of only one storey. But just the same the Parson and the rest would have plenty to do for quite a while.

Tex went to the office door and edged it open. The passage outside was empty and silent; so was the drinking saloon opposite, the door of which stood open.

He didn't waste any more time. He closed the door and locked it, leaving the window open as a means of escape should this become necessary. There was no light in the room, the oil-lamp, still smoking, providing evidence that the Parson had turned it out when he left. To light the lamp might be dangerous.

He went to the safe standing in the corner, out of sight of either window. His fingers manipulated the dials.

He heard the first ward click into place as he turned the dial. Those who didn't know him would have found it amazing that his great hands, muscular and strong, could be so sensitive.

It took him five minutes to open the safe. During that time he didn't move, didn't shift his posture. The last ward dropped into place. He turned the heavy handle and the door swung open.

Before he started in to investigate the contents, he slid to the Main Street window and peered out. He could see the fringe of the crowd round the burning saloon, could hear the confused noise, even the cracking of wood as the flames lapped hungrily. It seemed like attention was still concentrated on the saloon.

Tex went back to the safe. The first thing he took out was a ledger. He flicked over the pages rapidly.

CHAPTER 9

Tex was mighty interested in the ledger. Each page was headed by a name and a ranch. Some of the names Tex had already heard from Dave and Sam – there was Hackamore, for example, and there was Werner of the Block Diamond. Most he hadn't heard of, but it seemed that all the ranches in the district were listed, with dates and amounts in dollars entered in columns. This ledger contained the Parson's private record of the sums paid for protection.

Interesting, but an omission was even more interesting. Buck Forbes of the Lazy Y did not appear anywhere in the ledger. It was probable that his name was the only omission. In any event, even if this were not so, the fact that his name did not appear was significant.

It looked as though he was in with the guy, working in with him. In that case Linda's actions, in part, could be explained, including her defence of the Parson, including her anxiety to have Tex himself run out of town.

Tex stared at the ledger, trying to work things out. Take it that

Buck Forbes and the girl were in with the Parson, getting a cut of the profits, maybe. That would account for certain incidents, but not for all. It didn't account for her laying for him in the hills when he was after the Kid – provided that he was right over that and she had laid for him deliberately. Provided also that in doing so she'd aimed to give the Kid a hand.

Maybe she hadn't. There were several possibilities. She might have made a genuine mistake and thought he was one of the Kid's buddies; she might have realized who he was but not worked it out that her first shot would warn the Kid; she might be a sucker and not know that the Parson was a crook or that her cousin was in with him – if he was in fact operating this way.

Tex wanted to believe this, but he was honest with himself and knew that Linda Forbes wasn't a sucker. On the other hand he couldn't convince himself that she was crooked either. Maybe this was wishful thinking, he realized this. Crooks aren't always to be identified by their appearance. Linda looked a nice girl, but that needn't mean anything.

Tex gave it up, went back to the safe and stowed the ledger away carefully, in the exact position it had occupied before. He was making sure that the Parson didn't rumble that the safe had been opened.

The amounts paid to the Parson in the form of dues came to a respectable total. He was working a very profitable racket here. The fact that if Tex himself was ranching in these parts he'd see the guy dead before he parted with what amounted to blackmail dollars, didn't blind him to the fact that not many others would think along the same lines. Some might have found it unbelievable that folk would pay up to keep out of trouble, but not Tex. He'd seen the same racket worked in the cities, with property owners terrorized into paying. The racket could be worked all right given enough ruthless hoodlums on the pay-roll. It was being worked and the profits were large as Tex now knew.

He knew something else, too, after scrutinizing the ledgers. Not only were payments in recorded under the name of each ranch, but also payments out. These were listed under names. Tex could work it out easily enough. Cow-hands were being bribed by the Parson, bribed to stay quiet and do nothing. That made it sure that when any rancher decided to stick in his toes he'd get no help from his employees. The Parson had operated very slick.

The hotel remained deserted. Tex could still see the lurid light of the fire down Main Street and hear through the window the noise of the crowd. He still had time, he reckoned.

There was plenty of dough in the safe but Tex didn't touch it. There was a steel box which he opened, using a key hanging up in the safe itself. It was full of money. He didn't make anything of this until he started in examining another ledger, smaller than the first. What he found there interested him more even than the omission of Buck's name from the first ledger. There were entries indicating that the Parson's profits were not confined to the dues collected from ranchers. He'd recorded other items with meticulous accuracy. He'd taken ten grand from Buck Forbes during the past year, for instance; ten thousand dollars profit from poker playing with Buck. He'd collected a biggish sum from cattle deals, but not from legitimate selling of Double K stock, not according to the description of that ranch provided by Dave and Sam, corroborated by Pop Dwight. The Double K didn't own this number of cattle.

Tex remembered that when the Parson had first started operations cattle had been rustled, to prove that the territory needed protection from bandits. The Parson had cashed in both ways. Tex had no doubt the rustled cattle had been sold over the Mexican border – the dates worked in with that theory.

There was another item of interest before he reached the one that really got him thinking. Rod Werner, of the Block Diamond, had another page all to himself in this second ledger. On that page were entered various sums apparently paid by him over the last two years – not connected with the mutual protection racket, for otherwise why enter them in a separate ledger? There was a date alongside the entries, a date some ten years earlier. Tex made a note of it and of the total sum Werner had paid over to the Parson seemingly for nothing. There was a possible explanation which Tex tucked away in his mind for future consideration.

Then he came to the item which really held his attention. The last page of the ledger was a summary, a summary of what were stated to be profits for each quarter running back to the beginning of the Parson's operations. Each quarter's total was split into two. Then Tex remembered the steel box containing cash, separated from the rest in the safe.

He returned the ledger to the safe. There was nothing more of interest and he closed the heavy door. He was satisfied that every article had been replaced exactly where he had found it. There was nothing to show that the safe had been opened. It was a good piece of steel-work; Tex didn't reckon the Parson would suspect that anyone could open it without the combination. The odds were about a million to one against anyone else in the district having the necessary ability.

He was satisfied, too, with what he had discovered in the safe. There were items of interest, items to be considered carefully. But not right now. He'd done what he came to do and so far had been lucky, things had worked out the way he'd planned.

Going to the door of the office he turned the key in the lock. The Parson, no doubt in his hurry, had left it unlocked and must find it that way when he returned.

Then he made for the window. He was halfway to it when he heard tramping footsteps on the wooden verandah outside the hotel. Somebody was coming, and maybe to the office. Tex couldn't see out of the front window from where he was but he was taking no chances.

He made the window . . . and then ducked back swiftly. At the mouth of the alley were three guys standing, not ten yards from the window. Escape by that route was impossible without raising the alarm.

Tex ducked back, recrossed the office silently and reached the wall by the door. The footsteps were now coming along the passage outside. Tex brought out his gun and stood rigid against the wall so that if the door was opened it would cover him as it swung back.

The footseps halted outside the door. There wasn't much doubt now what was going to happen, and not much that it was the Parson out there. Somehow Tex didn't reckon that the Parson encouraged other guys to enter the office when he himself wasn't present.

But maybe the Parson had come back only to lock up, remembering he'd left the door unsecured. He'd have to come in, though, to get the key, which was on the inside. It looked like there was going to be a show-down.

The door swung open, covering him for a moment, as he'd estimated. Through the gap by the hinges Tex caught a glimpse of the Parson. He was alone, swung the door shut behind him and made towards his desk. There wasn't a hope of Tex being able to get out of the room unseen, or of taking cover.

He took a couple of steps to the side, so that he stood with his back to the closed door and brought up his gun. As the Parson swung round, hearing him move, he spoke.

'Take it easy . . . get your hands up, Parson.'

Tex knew he was taking a risk. If the Parson tried anything on, grabbed for his gun and fired, or started in shouting, the alarm would be raised. Tex could drop the Parson, but that wasn't the way he wanted to play this game. Tex had to keep the right side of the law if he could.

He was taking a risk, but he banked on the Parson being unwilling to take one.

'Get 'em up,' he repeated, 'I guess I can't miss at this range.'

The Parson got his hands up, making no attempt to grab for a gun. Tex went forward swiftly and relieved him of his rods.

'Now I reckon we can talk,' said Tex quietly. 'Sit down, Parson . . . you ain't got nothin' to worry about, I dropped in to have a talk with you, nice an' friendly, only when I got here you were up at the fire. I guess that's where you've been?'

'What do you want?' asked the Parson. 'You gone loco or somethin'? I got boys around, you can't get away with this.'

'There ain't anythin' I want to get away with. Don't take no notice o' the rod, that was a precaution . . . I wasn't aimin' to be put out by you. I want a friendly talk, like I said.'

He had already turned the key in the lock of the door. Now he crossed to the window at the front and drew the blind. He could do that without being seen from outside. The other window, giving on to the alley, was easier still, even with the guys standing at the Main Street end. Tex was hidden by the office wall as he drew down the cord.

'Now light the lamp,' he ordered. 'I can see you OK,' he added, 'so don't try on anythin', it won't pay.'

His gun covered the Parson as the latter fumbled with the matches Tex threw across to him and lit the oil lamp standing on the desk.

Tex drew out a chair and sat down opposite the Parson. His gun he allowed to rest on his knee. It was possible that some of the Parson's boys, now at the site of the fire, would return before he was through, but it was a chance he was taking. He could have got away all right when the Parson first entered the room, he could have looked after the guy and made sure he didn't raise the alarm; but Tex reckoned he'd got a better scheme than that. If he could convince him of something he could make good capital out of his unexpected arrival. The other way the Parson would have known for sure that he was on the trail and maybe have suspected that he'd tampered with the office – and the safe. Tex aimed to give him something else to think about and maybe at the same time reap another dividend.

'What you want?' asked the Parson again, his eyes not leaving Tex's face.

'Like I said, a friendly talk. You and me have got to get together, pal. I reckon we'd suit each other.' He paused and then added, 'Last night you got me all wrong, Parson. I don't say I'm blamin' you for that, but actin' hasty you got me wrong.'

'What you mean? You tellin' me you didn't stack the deck? Cut it out, mister, nobody takes dough from Spike without stackin'.'

'Sure, sure, I know that. I stacked the deck, but it was Spike's ace the dame found. It don't signify, I ain't interested in poker. I took Spike for a ride because I was aimin' to show you I got what it takes. I'd heard about you, Parson, I got ways an' means. I came down here to contact you. I wasn't reckonin' on bein' lynched. But I guess we can forget that. I'm willin' if you are.'

The Parson was interested all right, Tex knew that. There was a different expression in his eyes now. But he went on bluffing, which again Tex had expected.

'I don't get this,' he grunted. 'What's it matter to me you can stack a deck? I ain't got no interest in crooks.'

Tex allowed himself to smile.

'Come clean, Parson, there ain't no point in beatin' about the bush. You're workin' a pretty racket in these parts – several I reckon, not just the mutual protection racket. You worked out, I guess, maybe somebody had sent for me to try my hand breakin' it . . . you were right, Sam Steel contacted me an' asked me to come down. But you weren't right in reckonin' that I came to do what Sam asked. No, sir, I got more sense'n that. I've made a bit on the side durin' the last few years, a bit more'n I'd have made gettin' after bandits. Sam don't know that and neither does Dave, but it's a fact. When I got the dope about you I worked it out maybe you could use me – I ain't greedy but I could do with some dough. An' I guess I can be useful to a guy like you.'

The Parson had listened to this lot with what was obviously growing attention and interest. When Tex had finished he said nothing for a bit but sat there staring at him, eyes unwinking. Tex leaned back and hoped he'd pulled the bluff skilfully enough. One thing was pretty certain – that he'd given the guy something to think about, enough to take his mind off any thoughts regarding Tex's activities before the Parson entered the office.

'I've come clean,' Tex continued at last, breaking the silence. 'I'm lookin' for a job and maybe you can do with a guy like me. I could be useful, I reckon, seein' that nobody in these parts'll know I'm workin' in with you. Up at the Bar X they reckon I'm on the level.' He paused and then added, 'I know a mighty lot about you, Parson . . . there was cattle you sold. I guess it wasn't your cattle to sell. But don't get me wrong, I ain't aimin' to talk, not to anyone else. You can trust me.'

Then the Parson spoke.

'So you ain't on the level?'

'I'm out for what I can grab for myself,' was the reply. 'You tell me a sensible guy who ain't that way.'

The Parson shifted in his chair but stopped quickly when Tex moved his gun slightly.

'OK, I ain't tryin' anythin' on, take it easy, Scarron.' And then, 'You know quite a bit, don't you? Where'd you hear 'bout the cattle?' He paused as another thought occurred to him and added, 'How you get away last night, mister? I reckon maybe the Kid was hangin' around?'

Tex made up his mind swiftly. He didn't know for sure whether any of the Parson's boys had actually seen the Kid and recognized the bandit from his clothes. It could be that way. Tex wasn't taking the risk of lying.

'Sure, he was around,' he answered easily. 'He got me loose, but don't you go thinkin' I'm workin' in with the Kid, I ain't. I guess it ain't my habit to work in with anyone unless there's somethin' in it for me. The Kid cut me loose but I ain't got nothin' to do with the guy. I saw him a bit later when he was gunnin' against some other guys I didn't sight, but that's all.'

The Parson was silent for a bit. He still didn't like the idea of the Kid loose in the district, but he reckoned the Tex Scarron set-up was of more immediate importance. The Kid could wait, and maybe wouldn't ask for trouble by staying on in the territory. The Parson reckoned now, after more mature consideration, that probably he wouldn't hang around.

'Where'd you hear 'bout the cattle?' he asked again, abandoning the subject of the Kid, on the whole reckoning Tex had told the truth on that score.

'It don't signify. I get around. What you say – you got a job for me?'

'Maybe . . . sure, I guess I can use you.'

'That's fine. You'd best tell your boys to lay off me, then. I'll be more use alive than strung up. You can manage the bunch?'

The other's thick lips drew back. He could manage his bunch, yes.

'Don't let that keep you awake . . . the boys'll do what I tell 'em.'

Tex wasn't sure of him yet, didn't know whether he'd pulled off the bluff or whether in turn the Parson was bluffing him. But maybe it would work out all right. Before he could say anything else there came a commotion from Main Street, the clatter of horses hoofs and the grinding of wheels, which came to a halt outside the hotel.

Tex got to his feet swiftly.

'Have a look,' he ordered.

The Parson had to obey, with the gun menacing him. He left the desk and went to the front window, drawing aside the blind.

What he saw brought an oath to his lips, making him forget for the moment the Tex Scarron set-up.

The daily stage had drawn up outside the hotel and some of the crowd outside the burning saloon had detached themselves and were now gathered round the coach. The Parson saw Jeb and Snake, just coming out of the hotel. They must have been the guys he had heard entering a few minutes before. Now they were making for the stage.

The door of the vehicle was open and a solitary passenger was climbing out. It was the sight of this passenger that brought the oath to the Parson's lips. Climbing out with some difficulty was a huge, fat negress, frizzy black hair done up in a vivid scarlet bandanna, a print dress of no less vivid yellow swathing her ample proportions. Her face was wreathed in a gigantic smile, until stepping down to the street she slipped and fell.

There was a chorus of laughter from the bystanders and some catcalls from some of the boys. The negress got to her feet, mighty swiftly for one of her weight. As she did so her hand dug into a string bag she was carrying – and came out with a gun in it. She was smiling again now, but the gun was levelled menacingly. The spectators drew back involuntarily.

The Parson swore again at this scene which might have come out of a musical comedy. Then Tex spoke behind him.

'I'll be seein' you, Parson . . . I'm gettin' now. You think over what I've said. I'll contact you.'

With that he was by the side window. The alley was now deserted again. He swung over the sill and before the Parson could grab the guns which Tex had left on a side table after disarming him, was away, swallowed up by the shadows of the alley. When the Parson got to the window he was out of sight.

CHAPTER 10

Tex retrieved his pony, still where he had left it, undiscovered, and moved furtively back across the waste land west of the township. The fire was less bright now, for the building wasn't large enough to withstand the flames long.

That so far at all events the Parson had no suspicion that Tex had been responsible seemed certain. Fires in such settlements as Grant's River were common enough in summer. Tex hoped that he wouldn't come under suspicion, for if not there was a chance that the bluff he had pulled on the spur of the moment might pay dividends.

It might come off – only time would tell. In the meantime there had been achieved concrete results which must be considered – and used when this had been done. As he joined the minor trail which eventually led to the Bar X, Tex was thinking about these results.

The moon was well up by now. Tex rode along the trail towards the Bar X thinking hard. Part of his mind was wondering where Linda Forbes had been making when he had glimpsed her earlier. He was on the alert, but just the same Pop Dwight surprised him. The first he knew that Pop was around was when the latter spoke.

'OK, Tex . . . how'd you make out?'

Tex didn't answer until they were both under cover off the trail; and then he didn't go into details of his moves at the settlement.

'All right, I reckon . . . what you doin' here, Pop? I thought you were goin' up to the ranch?'

'Sure, but I didn't get there. Seems like I wasn't the only guy around these parts. I got a glimpse o' Doc Black. That was after I left you. I trailed him.'

Doc Black, up here near the Bar X. That might be something, though on the other hand it might mean nothing.

'Whcre'd he go?' asked Tex.

'I don't rightly know . . . he's pretty slick. I don't reckon he knew I was after him, but he could have done. Any road, he slipped me. I looked around but I didn't get a smell of him again. Then I saw Poston, he's the sheriff, remember? He came ridin' down the trail away from the Bar X. Maybe he paid a visit up there. He made towards the River. I let him go and scouted round for Black, but he ain't shown up again.'

Tex grunted, not knowing what to make of this. The trail was mostly used by Bar X guys and others needing to visit the ranch, but it led also to the foothills and other grazing grounds farther west. Tex didn't need to be reminded that Poston was the sheriff. Maybe he had been to the ranch. If so Sam and Dave would have looked after him – but given nothing away. As for Black he might have visited the Bar X, too. And there was Linda Forbes, who apparently Pop hadn't seen.

Before Tex could talk both he and Pop heard the noise of hoofs coming down the trail from the direction of the ranch. A couple of minutes later they saw who was coming, the moonlight revealing a rider whose shoulder sagged.

'The Doc,' muttered Pop. 'What's he been doin' up here?'

Tex didn't know. He watched the guy with interest. He was small and neatly built, but the sagging, crippled left shoulder lent him a grotesque air, gave him almost the appearance of a hunchback. The moonlight revealed a pallid face heavily lined, the cheekbones prominent.

Clouds were unexpectedly banking up in the sky. Even as they watched the Doc approach and draw level with where they were hiding up, the moon disappeared and the night was dark. They could no longer see the Doc plainly but they could hear him as he moved on down the trail. After a little the noise of his progress ceased – a bit earlier than it should have done, Tex judged. It seemed like the Doc might have turned off the trail on to grass.

Then, in the distance, coming towards them but from the direction of Grant's River, not the ranch, they heard the sound of another pony, certainly not the Doc's. The sound drew nearer and then the moon flicked out from behind the clouds again. Not for long, but long enough to reveal that the sheriff was coming along the trail towards them.

Their guns ready in case of accidents, Tex and Pop waited and watched. There was a whole lot of interest being displayed in this Bar X ground tonight.

They saw Poston, slouched in the saddle the way he always rode, shoulders hunched, his nondescript face grey under the moon, rein in. Then he turned his horse off the trail and struck north.

'We'll have a look-see,' said Tex. 'I guess they ain't either of 'em up here pickin' daisies. Better split . . . make back to the Bar X if you don't get anythin'.'

Then minutes later Tex, once more on his own, was moving cautiously between outcrops that here jagged above the surface of the ground dividing two of the Bar X grazing grounds. The land here was mostly good pasture, but there was a pocket of outcrops and scattered rocks. After leaving Pop, Tex had reckoned he'd glimpsed somebody moving in this direction and he had followed along, as cautiously as he could. The moon was still concealed, but the night was by no means pitch dark.

Whoever he'd seen, provided that it hadn't been a coyote prowling, had gone. There was neither sight nor sound of him. Tex reined in amongst the outcrops, ears strained. Where Pop was he didn't know. He'd gone after the sheriff. It seemed like Tex was all alone.

But then he heard a noise pretty close at hand. Somebody was approaching, must have been riding across pasture, all sound deadened, until now, when whoever it was must have entered the stony terrain of the outcrops. Tex was remembering the Kid right then.

His gun came out. He backed his pony under the shelter of a rearing boulder and waited. He hadn't got a clue who was coming, nor why the Doc and the sheriff were lurking about up here.

The noise came nearer, a pony's hoofs scrabbling on loose stones. Then without warning the moon came out again. The moonlight revealed who it was approaching – Linda Forbes. It also revealed Tex to her.

The girl reined in, startled. Her hand moved involuntarily to the gun at her waist, but then she saw Tex's Colt, in his hand, and made no other movement.

Tex touched his pony and moved up to her.

'Evenin',' he drawled. 'Seems like we're always meetin'. But maybe you didn't expect to see me? Guess you thought I was swingin' high an' dry by now?'

'I didn't mean . . . I didn't know they'd try lynchin',' she said in a low voice.

'No? But you reckoned I ought to be run out o' town? Sure . . . but you got it all wrong. Do I look like a card sharp?'

A little colour crept into her cheeks.

'I don't know what you look like.'

He waited for more but it didn't come. She wasn't looking at him, kept her eyes away.

'You got it all wrong,' he said. 'I've had a talk with the Parson, we understand each other now, I guess. I explained he'd been a bit hasty, an' you, too . . . we'll get along all right now, I guess. He's a nice guy when you get to know him.'

He watched her closely as he spoke. Without saying anything definite he'd given a clear indication that from now on he aimed to work in with the Parson; a clear indication, supposing that she knew that the Parson was crooked, that he was from now on in the racket himself.

She looked up at that – Tex could see that the hint had got home. And that, he judged, was in turn evidence that she did know all about the Parson.

'You're goin' to join up with the Parson?' she asked.

'Sure, we'll get along all right. I thought maybe you'd like to know that. You an' me needn't quarrel now, so long as you take my word I didn't use that extra ace. If the Parson is willin' to accept that I guess you can?'

The way she'd spoken her last question meant a lot to Tex. It wasn't just the words she'd used but the tone she employed. She knew what the Parson was all right. Now, when she spoke again, his hunch was reinforced.

'Of course . . . if the Parson says you're OK that's all right by me. I'm sorry I got you wrong.'

As she spoke she moved slightly in the saddle. For the first time Tex saw something that sharpened his interest. Down one sleeve of her shirt were stains – bloodstains, streaking the fabric.

He said nothing about them, but noticed that the girl made a movement to cover the sleeve. She was definitely paler than usual; and now he realized that the hand holding the reins of her pony was shaking a little as it lay on the saddle-bow.

She didn't seem to be injured, but where had the blood-stains come from? Tex was mighty interested, but he made no reference to them. It often paid to keep quiet. She didn't know he'd seen the blood.

He didn't need to ask the question that he had intended to put; she answered it without that.

'I've been ridin',' she said. 'I needed some air. I'd best be gettin' now.'

So she'd been riding just for air and exercise? Tex wasn't swallowing that but again he kept quiet. Instead of querying the statement he asked another question.

'You ain't seen anyone around, except me?' he asked.

'No . . . I've seen nobody.'

The answer was sharp, the voice taut. She flashed him a glance which seemed to him to be one of apprehension. Then she looked away again abruptly. There was no doubt she was on edge, strung up, upset about something – and that something wasn't just meeting up with him. There was no doubt either that she had lied about not seeing anyone. She'd seen somebody all right. She wasn't so hot at bluffing.

Tex let her go, watching her out of sight, making for the Bar X trail. She'd given him plenty to think about. He had no concrete evidence but he was dead sure on certain matters. She hadn't been riding just for the pleasure of it; she knew what the Parson was; she'd either met or at least seen somebody up here near the Bar X. Again he was remembering the Kid.

He was dead sure about all these matters. And there were the bloodstains on her shirt sleeve. Maybe they were old stains, maybe they had been picked up by accident and innocently . . . but maybe not. Tex sure had plenty to think about.

He abandoned any idea of getting on the trail of Doc Black. He turned his pony and cut back to the trail, aiming for the Bar X. Sam and Dave would be waiting pretty anxiously to know how he had made out at the hotel. The ranch was still nearly two miles distant.

Half a mile from the ranch, which was, however, still hidden from view, he met up with Pop Dwight again. Pop had not been lucky. He hadn't got a smell of Poston, had spent some time scouting around but then had called it a day and made back to the Bar X.

'OK, we'll have a talk with Sam and Dave,' said Tex.

'You have any luck?' asked Pop.

'Maybe . . . I met up with Linda Forbes. Seems she was ridin' for her health, so she said.'

'Linda? Heck, what was she. . . ?'

Pop didn't complete the remark, for by now they had come within view of the Bar X, and what he saw effectually stopped Pop.

The ranch-house was streaming with lights, which streamed out into the night, illuminating a group of guys gathered round something lying on the ground at one corner of the building. The bunkhouse, nearby, was standing with its door open and there were other guys, Bar X cowhands, gathered there.

Tex and Pop put their ponies into a canter, came up to the house swiftly. As they came Sam Steel detached himself from the group, which opened up. Then it could be seen that someone lay on the ground. It was Dave Brand.

Pop Dwight let fall an oath as he saw the knife sticking out of Dave's back, blood congealing on the stuff of his check shirt.

Then Sam was with them, face set.

'Dave's handed in his checks . . . I found him five minutes ago, like this. He was dead, knifed in the back.'

Tex swung from the saddle, made his way to where Dave Brand lay. He didn't need to check Sam's report. Tex had seen plenty of dead men in his time. Dave was gone all right, murdered.

He stared down at the old man, remembering how good he had been to him in the old days of boyhood. Tex was remembering something else, too . . . the bloodstains on Linda Forbes's shirt sleeve.

Tex was still thinking about the bloodstains when he helped to carry Dave into the house.

CHAPTER 11

The two men sat in the Parson's office at the hotel, the Parson himself smoking a cigar, the other, Doc Black, chewing rhythmically. The Doc's face was as pallid as ever, even in the strong afternoon sun which slanted through the office window, the expression as saturnine. He sat with his back to the front window, so that the sun silhouetted him, throwing into relief his sagging shoulder, picking out the grotesque lines of his crippled body.

It was the afternoon following the killing of Dave Brand up at the Bar X. As a result of that the Parson had been given plenty to think about; and right now he was doing some thinking. He and the Doc had been talking for some time.

'What you know 'bout this dame callin' herself Bluebell?' asked the Doc after a pause which followed the lengthy discussion of the murder of Dave Brand. 'I guess she pulled a fast one buyin' up old man Graw.'

At the mention of the negress who had busted into Grant's River so dramatically on the previous evening, the Parson drew back his lips. He'd had plenty to think about since Dave's killing, but that hadn't prevented him taking steps with regard to Bluebell, as she called herself. She sure had pulled a fast one, buying up Bill Graw's general store which was situated right opposite the hotel. The Parson hadn't even known Graw was pulling out. According to Bluebell she'd bought the property through a Phoenix solicitor. Bill Graw had sold furtively and had cleared.

The Parson didn't like it. He'd been aiming to get his hands on the store for a long time but Graw wouldn't sell. The Parson had reckoned to force him, but he'd put it off, and now he'd missed his chance. The store belonged to the negress, all legal, as the Parson had discovered, and Bill Graw had cleared, escaping retribution.

The Parson turned and stared out of the window. Bluebell, still clad in vivid yellow, with the scarlet bandana round her frizzy hair, was standing on a ladder busily engaged in repainting the legend over the shop. Bill Graw's name had been obliterated and the negress had nearly completed a new sign. Even as the Parson watched she finished the name BLUEBELL and started drawing in decorative lines underneath. Half a dozen loafers were standing around watching her, but it was noticeable that they weren't shooting off any wisecracks. They were mighty courteous when they did speak.

The Doc followed the Parson's eyes, taking in the scene framed by the window.

'They tell me she's tough,' he said.

The Parson growled in his throat. On the previous evening Bluebell had startled Grant's River, even making the inhabitants who witnessed her arrival in the stage forget for the time being about the fire at the saloon. They hadn't expected a stranger to come busting in, they hadn't expected the store to change hands; and certainly they hadn't anticipated a negress with a gun in her hand. It certainly seemed that Bluebell was tough. Snake had been along to talk to her since then, and according to him she'd refused to play ball over the mutual protection scheme.

The Parson stubbed out his cigar. He'd get around to dealing with her pretty soon. The store was a good proposition, no doubt about that. Bill Graw had made a packet out of it; and the Parson had aimed to do the same when he got hold of the place. He'd been hi-jacked, though. If he could get his hands on Graw, who had pulled a fast one, clearing without anyone knowing he was going, he'd teach him a thing or two. He couldn't touch Graw now, but he could get at Bluebell. She'd pay up, all right, and she wouldn't be staying in Grant's River, the Parson would make sure of that.

But first there were other matters to be attended to, one in particular. He brushed aside the subject of the newcomer. Like Tex on the previous night he reckoned she wasn't all that important. And also like Tex that was his mistake.

'I guess we got somethin' else to talk about,' he grunted.

The Doc got to his feet. He was short and his crippled shoulder made him seem even shorter, so that even when he was standing he didn't stand so much higher than the Parson still seated at the desk. But for all his lack of stature there was something about Doc Black, more than a suggestion, of power.

'That's settled, ain't it? There ain't nothin' else to talk about. It'll work out. I got to be goin'.'

He went towards the door and then turned back for a moment.

'I ain't thanked you for the dough. We're doin' all right.' And then, slowly, 'We got to make sure o' this guy Scarron this time, Parson.'

The Parson didn't answer. When the Doc had gone he continued sitting at the desk, fingering a fresh cigar but not lighting it. He was thinking about good dollars spent out, a heck of a lot of dollars; he was thinking about Tex Scarron and the murder of Dave Brand . . . he was thinking about Doc Black, who was a clever guy, no doubt about that. Sure, a clever guy, who'd brought working undercover to a fine art.

His glance travelled to Main Street again. Bluebell had come down from her ladder now, was standing there with a paint-pot in one hand, a brush in the other. Round her capacious waist was a belt containing a Colt, very prominent. As he watched the Parson saw her hand the pot to one of the loafers, who took it and went into the shop with it. Bluebell stood laughing with the others, her shining ebony face wreathed in smiles. The Parson couldn't hear what she said, but the guys were laughing, too. It seemed like she was getting on the right side of the River residents.

She'd better be happy while she could be, reflected the Parson sardonically. He'd attend to her and he hoped pretty soon. Then he saw somebody come into view down the hotel steps, standing for a moment watching the group on the other side of the street and finally move away out of sight. The Parson watched the retreating back of Pop Dwight until the guy disappeared from view. He sat quite still, and now he wasn't thinking about anyone but Pop, owner of the *Gazette*. Involuntarily the Parson's eyes narrowed. One hand clenched, the other, holding the cigar, moved restlessly, twisting it to and fro. He knew Pop had been in the hotel, sure he knew, because he'd talked to him. And even when he was talking to the Doc, when he was thinking about other matters, including the murder at the Bar X and the fire at the drinking saloon, the thought of Pop Dwight had still nibbled at his mind.

For a long time after Pop had passed from sight the Parson continued to sit at his desk, sorting out his thoughts and his plans. Things had begun to go wrong since the guy Scarron had blown in. On the previous evening the Parson hadn't been sure about Tex. He'd thought that maybe he was on the level with him, but he knew better now. He'd had word, sure word that the guy had been bluffing, must have been. He wasn't in these parts aiming to cut in on the rackets. He was here to bust them wide open . . . and he was dangerous, pretty well-known. He'd got to be liquidated. The scheme to do this seemed OK to the Parson, even though given his head he'd have gone about it another way, using more direct methods. But thinking it over he reckoned that the more subtle manoeuvre, put up to him during the last hour, would be better. Sure . . . the guy who'd put it up had brains, that was certain.

OK then Scarron could be liquidated. That would leave the Parson sitting pretty again . . . except for the fifty per cent cut he had to pay out every quarter. It hurt him every time he thought about that. He'd just paid out the last quarter's cut; maybe there wouldn't be another payment made. Once Scarron was out of the way the Parson could get down to something he'd been thinking about for some long time. Fifty per cent was too much . . . anything was too much. He reckoned he could work it.

His thoughts were interrupted by a knock on the door. When it opened there was the rat-faced Snake, with Werner of the Block Diamond behind him, towering over Snake, a tall lath of a man, sullen of face, furtive of eye.

'You got a visitor, boss,' said Snake.

'OK, beat it . . . come in, Werner, I've been expectin' you.'

Werner shuffled into the room, closing the door behind him. He thrust one hand into his pocket and brought out a wad of dirty dollars.

'Your dough,' he muttered, putting the dollars down on the desk.

The Parson took the dollars and checked them through. Then he looked up.

'You're a hundred short,' he said.

'I know, but I ain't got any more to spare.'

The Parson fiddled with the bills, thick underlip protruding.

'That's OK, Werner, I guess it don't matter to me if the Governor hears what you were doin' one night ten years ago . . . there's a new Governor, guess you've heard that? He don't go big they say for . . .'

The man interrupted him violently.

'You ain't goin' to talk, Parson. I've paid up regular until now . . . you got to give me a break. I tell you I ain't got the dough. You don't leave me enough to live on, Parson.'

The Parson was thinking pretty fast. He'd done well out of Werner; a hundred dollars didn't make much difference to him. Werner could be useful.

'OK, we'll forget the hundred,' he said. 'I guess I'll be wantin' your help, though.'

Werner fell for that, as the Parson had known he would. A few minutes later the Parson was alone again, one small detail of the scheme to liquidate Tex Scarron settled.

He wasn't alone long, though, for Snake came sliding in, closing the door behind him.

'What you want?' demanded the Parson. 'I don't reckon I sent for you.'

'That's right, boss, but I got somethin' to say. I guess you ought to listen.'

The Parson stared at him. He'd always known that Snake had more brains than the rest of the bunch of hoodlums he kept employed. Lately he'd been wondering about Snake. It had seemed to the Parson that the guy had something on his mind. Now maybe he was going to let out what it was.

'What is it?' he asked.

Snake looked at the door, went across to it and turned the key.

'It's kinda private,' he murmured. The close-set eyes were bright and intelligent, the thin lips curved in a half-smile. 'Sure, kinda private,' he repeated. 'I been thinkin' about the fifty per cent cut you hand out.'

That brought the Parson up standing. He stood motionless, eyes not leaving Snake's face.

'What do you mean?' he asked at last.

Snake shrugged his shoulders.

'I reckon we can forget that, boss. I know you hand out a cut to the guy who's in with you. I been usin' my eyes. You got somebody in with you . . . and it costs you plenty, don't it?'

The Parson took time off to light his cigar, giving himself a long interval while he thought. His mind was moving quickly. Snake wasn't bluffing, he dismissed that idea almost before it was formed. Snake knew that he had a partner . . . OK, maybe that fact could be used to advantage. The Parson's mind wasn't as quick as the guy's who had been behind him ever since he came to Grant's River, who had put up the cash necessary to buy the Double K and finance the various rackets, but he had a brain and could use it. He was using it right now. Snake's entrance had come pat on his own thoughts that fifty per cent was too much; that anything was too much. Snake might be useful.

The Parson didn't try any bluffing. He got straight down to business.

'So you know 'bout that? Who else knows? Jeb, maybe?'

Snake's thin lips drew back farther.

'Jeb don't know nothin'. Nobody don't know but me.'

The Parson nodded. Jeb was useful for his strength, but he was about as dumb as a beeve.

'OK, Snake, you know a lot . . ..you know who my partner is?'

Snake didn't hesitate. The Parson reckoned he was telling the truth. There wasn't any reason he could see why he should lie.

'That's somethin' I ain't got around to yet. I worked it out maybe we could do a deal.'

They were getting somewhere now.

'What sort o' deal?'

Snake rolled himself a cigarette. Nobody smoked in the office without the Parson's permission, but now he let it go. He wasn't falling out with Snake.

'You like payin' out all that dough, boss?' asked Snake, when he had lit the cigarette. 'I guess I wouldn't go big for it. Seems kinda wasteful, don't it?'

The Parson agreed – he'd been thinking along the same lines for quite a while. By now he knew just why Snake had brought up the subject. He was hoping there'd be something in it for him. How he'd got on to the truth the Parson didn't know. Snake knew that there was somebody behind him and that was all that mattered – to the Parson. Snake could be used and then discarded.

'Sure, kinda wasteful,' he repeated. 'I been thinkin' that, Snake. What's your proposition?'

Snake blew a stream of smoke.

'I reckon maybe we could get rid o' the guy? Sure, why not . . . you cut me in, boss, an' I'll give him the works. I reckon maybe he takes precautions with you,' he added shrewdly, 'but not knowin' I'm on to him maybe he won't worry about me.'

Again he had repeated the Parson's thoughts. Sure, Snake could be useful.

'Cut you in? I ain't payin' out fifty per cent to nobody else.'

'Sure you ain't. My proposition is ten per cent, I ain't greedy, boss, not like some guys.'

The Parson inhaled cigar smoke. Snake's proposition was OK for the time being. Once the job was done, though, he needn't think he was going to cash in for the rest of his natural. He could be got rid of at leisure.

To use him to get the guy who had taken fifty per cent cut for so long was OK. The Parson had played around with the idea lately, but like Snake had said, his partner didn't take any risks when he was with the Parson. For all the fact that nobody else in Grant's River reckoned he was dangerous, not knowing he was in with the Parson, the latter knew just how dangerous he was. He wasn't scared of many guys, but this one was dangerous. The Parson wanted him out of the way but so far he hadn't worked up the nerve to try it on. He hadn't thought of recruiting anyone to help him; but now Snake had done the thinking for him.

'OK, that's a deal,' he said at last.

'Fine, you goin' to put a name to the guy?'

That wasn't the Parson's idea, not yet. Later he'd have to, but he was aiming to leave that until the last moment. He wasn't running the risk of Snake getting along to the guy and maybe making a deal with him.

'I'll come to that later,' he said. 'You keep your mouth shut . . . we got to settle with this guy Scarron first.'

Snake didn't press the question of the unknown's name. He could bide his time and knew the Parson didn't mean to talk yet. He agreed that Scarron had got to be liquidated. Snake knew a dangerous guy when he saw him.

'You goin' to bump him off, boss?' And then, 'What about Dave Brand? Who used a knife on him last night?'

The Parson smiled slowly.

'I guess that was Scarron,' he said. 'He was down here last night. Sure, an' he fired the saloon . . . he had plenty o' time after leavin' here to attend to Dave up at the Bar X.'

Snake's eyes were like slits as he stared back at the Parson. Word had come to the River that Dave Brand had been knocked off, knifed. The sheriff had ridden up to the ranch that morning, as Snake knew, had come back and reported to the Parson. Snake knew also that Tex Scarron was up at the ranch, had apparently been lying up there. But it was a new one on him that he'd killed Dave. It didn't make sense, he reckoned.

'Sure, he did the killin',' said the Parson easily. 'Lucky he did, maybe, it'll put him where he belongs.'

Snake nodded slowly. He was getting there now.

'I reckon so, boss. It'll put him away nice an' neat. You reckon you can work it?'

He obviously wasn't swallowing the tale that Tex had killed Dave, but the Parson wasn't worrying. He reckoned his partner had been right in working it this way to get Tex. He was a very slick guy, this newcomer; ordinary murder might not come off. He knew how to look after himself. But he wouldn't be expecting the sort of move which would be taken, nor the way it would be initiated. The trap would be sprung cleverly.

There was another advantage, as the Parson had to admit. Arresting a guy on a murder charge, with evidence against him, and then shooting him when he tried to get away, was better than bumping him off without any excuse. Sure, anyone was entitled to shoot in self-defence against a murderer trying to escape. The incident could be made all neat and tidy – and legal.

'You got it taped, boss?' asked Snake. 'How you know the timin' is OK? Maybe the guy's got an alibi.'

The Parson wasn't worrying about that, nor about Snake being let in on the scheme. Snake was in with him now, aiming to get his ten per cent cut. He was to be trusted . . . while it suited him, which would be for a bit yet.

'I got it taped,' he said. 'I get information OK.'

Snake thumbed out his cigarette. He'd got brains all right. The Parson was getting information – from the Bar X obviously, or from somebody who knew what had happened up there.

'Maybe Brady's been earnin' his dough?' he suggested.

'Sure, Brady's useful.'

Brady was a cowhand at the Bar X. Snake knew he'd been on the Parson's pay-roll for some time. Another thought occurred to Snake.

He wasn't swallowin' the tale that Scarron had put out Dave Brand; that meant that somebody else had. It couldn't have been the Parson, because according to Doc Black, who had been taken up by Poston to view the body, Dave had been killed during the time the Parson was at the settlement, the fire still smouldering. Snake himself had been at the fire, had seen most of the Parson's boys there.

'What you know?' he asked briefly, watching the Parson.

The Parson understood what he meant but he wasn't talking.

'I told you – Scarron did the killin', Snake. We got evidence. Don't you go thinkin' this is a frame-up, that wouldn't be sensible, I guess. An' maybe it wouldn't be safe . . . get me?'

Sure Snake got him. He didn't underrate the Parson. He'd struck a bargain with him but Snake wasn't taking any risks. Maybe it would be more important to the Parson to shut his mouth about the Scarron case than use him against the unknown partner. Snake wouldn't talk. Scarron was dangerous and he was all for putting him away.

'I get you boss,' he said. 'I'm mighty glad you got evidence against Scarron, we don't want no murderers around here. He ain't got wind o' what's intended?'

'He's sittin' tight up at the Bar X . . . there's somethin' else, Snake. He gets the property now Brand has handed in his checks. That's a strong motive, I reckon. Don't you worry, he's up there an' he'll stay there. The sheriff'll be ridin' to get him along with a posse before long. He'll be there, he don't know he's been rumbled. You keep your mouth shut.'

'Sure, boss. . . .'

He was interrupted by a commotion from outside. Then somebody rattled at the door of the office.

When the Parson opened it he was confronted by a group of his boys in the passage outside. Jeb was there and Rocky Schultz and half a dozen others. Somebody else was there, too – Bluebell, held by Jeb and Rocky. She looked dishevelled, the bandanna all awry, yellow dress crumpled. Jeb was holding a gun in his hand.

'Gee, boss, this dame came bustin' in,' said Jeb, 'I guess. . . .'

Bluebell broke into a torrent of words, her face shining with anger.

'Ah'm a respectable woman,' she screamed at the Parson. 'Let me tell you Ah'm not in the habit o' bein' mishandled by a set o' these hoodlums you keep around the place.'

It was some time before the Parson could get to the facts. Then he found that Bluebell had busted into the hotel demanding to see the Parson. She'd pulled a gun. It hadn't been so easy to get her under control.

'I reckon she's loco,' said Jeb, fondling his face where her black fist had struck him.

'Ah'm not loco,' stated Bluebell. 'Ah've come to tell you, mister,' to the Parson, 'that Ah ain't payin' no protection dollars. You get that straight . . . Bluebell don't pay nothin' to nobody.'

She stuck her arms akimbo, fists on massive hips and faced the Parson, contemptuous of the guns now menacing her.

'You got that? You start sendin' any more guys like him,' jerking her head at Snake, 'and Ah'll riddle 'em. Ah can look after myself without no protection . . . you'll find that out, mister, if you try anythin' on.'

The Parson stared at her balefully. Then, as she suddenly raised one ham-like hand, he backed away swiftly.

A great grin cracked open Bluebell's face.

'That's better, Ah guess a lot o' guys have felt my fist.'

From the back of the crowd now in the office there came a laugh. The Parson swung round, face dark with anger.

'Any other guy who cracks his face won't have no face to crack,' he snarled. Then to Jeb, 'Get her out o' here. . . .'

They hustled Bluebell out, but not before a few of them had felt the weight of her fists. The Parson was left alone. It took him some little time to recover his self-possession sufficiently to have Poston brought in and make final arrangements with him to take a posse up to the Bar X.

That posse would be made up mainly of the Parson's boys, but there'd got to be a few others to make it look on the level. Doc Black would be one of them, and Werner another. It was an easy way to earn a hundred bucks, the Parson reckoned.

Strangely enough, or maybe not strangely considering how many other things he had to think about, the Parson hadn't taken any time off to wonder whether the Kid was still around the place and if so what he was doing. That was his mistake, the second at least that he'd made.

CHAPTER 12

Up at the Bar X late that afternoon things were pretty gloomy with old Dave lying dead in his bedroom. Death had come to the ranch furtively, murderously, and its miasma hung over the place.

Both Sam and Tex took it hard, Sam harder than his friend, for though Dave had been Tex's uncle, nearly related to him, it was Sam who had seen so much of the old man, had lived and worked with him. Sam went around with a set face; for once he neglected ordinary range duties. It looked like the bottom had dropped out of his world, at least for the time being.

Since the death guys had ridden up to the Bar X, including the sheriff and Doc Black. The Doc had put the killing at some time within the hour preceding Sam's discovery of the body, he couldn't get nearer than that, which wasn't very helpful. The sheriff had asked questions but apparently hadn't got anywhere. He'd questioned Tex carefully about his movements that evening and up to a point, but only up to a point, Tex had told him the facts. He'd said that he'd been down to the River and talked to the Parson – implying as he had done to Linda, that he was from now on working in with the Parson. Sam hadn't been present when he pulled this one. Tex had stated that on the way back he met Pop Dwight, but that was all. He said nothing about seeing Linda Forbes nor about the sight they'd had of Doc Black and Poston himself. Pop wouldn't talk, Tex had put him up to that soon after the murder had been discovered.

Eventually the sheriff had ridden away, taking the Doc with him. He hadn't said anything about the near-lynching incident nor about the card sharping down at the hotel. Tex took it that maybe the Parson had already had a word with him; maybe he had told the sheriff that he'd gained a new recruit and warned Poston to lay off. The enquiries could be just for the look of the thing. There wasn't any proof yet that the Parson had swallowed Tex's bluff down at the hotel, but it could be that way. Tex hoped so.

The morning dragged by. Sam went down to the settlement to have a look around and pick up any gossip that was going. Tex stayed at the ranch, which as he realized when Dave's papers were examined, was now his property. Dave had left it to him, having no other relations. Sam's first thought after Tex and Pop had reached the Bar X after the murder was that Tex must stay. There was even more reason now than before. The protection racket had been bad enough, but the murder of old Dave was worse. Sam wanted retribution handed out. Tex had got to stay.

'I reckon you'll do that?' he asked anxiously.

Tex didn't hesitate. Sure he'd stay – and he'd get the guy who'd bumped off Dave. He spent some time while Sam was out looking around and questioning the cowhands who had been in the bunkhouse during the vital hour on the previous evening. From them he didn't learn much of importance because they'd been taking their leisure, playing poker or lying around listening to a guy who was pretty good with the guitar. There'd evidently been quite a row going on in the bunkhouse. None of them had heard anything. Nor had the cook, who had been in the ranch-house kitchen asleep.

Tex knew from Sam much of what had happened. Dave and Sam had been together in the living-room, talking, when Sam thought he heard a noise outside on the verandah. He'd slipped out to have a look-see, had glimpsed a vague shadow and had gone after whoever it was. He'd lost the guy but had scouted for him. He'd been gone some time, moving around the home corral and going farther afield when he thought he saw somebody moving across the home grazing-grounds. Eventually he'd returned to the ranch-house. He had stumbled over Dave lying there with a knife in his back. Dave must have left the house at some time after Sam. He had been attacked and killed. Sam had found the body only five minutes before Tex and Pop had arrived, but he'd been scouting around for some long time before then, at least half an hour he reckoned, maybe more, so there was no telling exactly when Dave was bumped off.

When Sam got back from the River he brought one item of information that interested Tex. Sam had learned, by casual conversation, that Buck Forbes had been away from the Lazy Y during the previous evening – and he hadn't been down at the hotel or the gambling saloon farther down Main Street.

'Maybe he was up here killin' Dave,' grunted Sam.

There was no reason to suppose this, but Sam was in the mood to suspect anyone, apparently. He was on edge, looking desperately for revenge and as he said angry with himself for leaving Dave alone. If he hadn't gone off scouting Dave would be alive right now.

Tex did what he could to convince him that this was hay-wire thinking, but Sam refused to be comforted.

'I guess it ain't no use talkin',' he said. 'Talk don't get you nowhere.'

Tex liked action all right, but he knew that sometimes talk was necessary. After they'd eaten at midday he got around to talking. By that time Pop Dwight had arrived at the Bar X. He'd spent part of the night at the ranch, but then had returned to the River. Now he was back – and Tex got down to the talk Sam didn't reckon was any use. There were a whole lot of leads and they had to be discussed. Some of them, one in particular, neither Sam nor Pop yet knew anything about. And nobody had any idea why Dave had been bumped off. Tex himself could only guess. He didn't like guessing, but at the moment that was all that could be done. But it was necessary to sort out the tangle of leads as well as he could.

He got Sam and Pop into the living-room, locked the door, and then got down to business.

'I reckon we got to talk,' he grunted. 'I been doin' some thinkin' this morning. We'll start from the beginnin'. I went down to the hotel last night like we arranged. I'll give you that first.'

He described what had happened at the settlement and the hotel, briefly recounting how he had ensured that the hotel should be emptied so that he could have a look inside the Parson's safe. He went on to explain what he had found and how the Parson had interrupted him.

'I pulled a bluff,' he added, 'and maybe it worked out. I ain't sure 'bout that yet.'

Sam and Pop didn't interrupt him but listened with close attention, this being the first opportunity Tex had of explaining the hotel work-out.

'OK, so there you have it,' continued Tex. 'Buck Forbes don't pay any dues, it seems, but he's been losin' very heavy to the Parson at poker. Werner, the guy who owns the Block Diamond, he's been payin' the Parson regular over and above the protection dues. I've got a hunch 'bout that . . . maybe he's bein' blackmailed. And the Parson is mighty careful to split his profits into two . . . sure, that's interestin'.'

'I don't get it,' muttered Sam. 'And it ain't got nothin' to do with the killin'. The Parson didn't bump off Dave 'ccordin' to you – he was down at the River.'

'Sure, an' he stayed there after you left, Tex, I got that hard,' contributed Pop. 'I went along to the hotel this mornin', had a look around an' a talk with the Parson an' some o' the boys. He was down there all night. The fire set him back.'

'He got any idea I started it?' asked Tex.

'I didn't get that far, the Parson's canny. Maybe he's on to you, maybe he ain't . . . but there was somethin' I did get. It could be important.'

Pop broke off, staring out of the window at a cowhand walking across to the bunkhouse, a short, stubby guy.

'There's Brady,' he continued slowly. 'He was down at the hotel this mornin'. He don't know I saw him, an' neither does the Parson. He was with the Parson an' he took some dollars from him.'

Sam gave an exclamation. Brady had been with the Bar X outfit for just over a year. He'd come from south of the border, so he'd stated when Dave took him on. Sam liked him well enough, he'd always been efficient.

'You reckon he's in with the Parson?' he demanded.

'Could be – he was takin' dough. Brady gets around, I've noticed him up here a few times slidin' about kinda furtive. If he is in with the Parson maybe your bluff won't work, Tex, not if Brady knows for sure you're on the level an' told the Parson. You talked 'bout what you meant to do down at the hotel last night . . . we ain't sure Brady didn't listen-in.'

Tex said nothing for a bit. There was no cast-iron proof that Brady was in with the Parson, only surmise that he had listened-in to the plans laid before Tex went to the hotel, but just the same it was something to be borne in mind.

Sam reckoned so, too. The house was wooden, eavesdropping was by no means impossible. When plans had been discussed nothing had been said about Tex starting a fire to get the guys out of the hotel, but the idea of busting open the Parson's safe had been fully discussed. If the Parson had been told that much it wasn't likely he'd go big for Tex's bluff.

'Guess we got to watch Brady,' he muttered.

'Sure, but it ain't important at the moment. If the Parson's on to me it don't matter all that, he won't get me again. I want to get back to the killin'.'

There were leads. Pop had seen Doc Black and had trailed him but lost him. Then he'd seen Poston, riding from the direction of the Bar X. Either of them Sam might have glimpsed a bit later after he'd left Dave in the living-room. Both Tex himself had seen after he'd met up with Pop again on leaving the settlement. One of the guys could have bumped off Dave, or both of them working together.

'Sure, but I don't get why,' muttered Pop. 'Dave paid the Parson his dough, what'd he want to set his boys on him for?'

Tex didn't know, didn't know for sure yet that Doc Black was in with the Parson, though it looked that way considering everything, remembering that the Doc had been up in the foothills when the gun battle against the Kid was in progress. Tex reckoned the sheriff was certainly in with the Parson.

Maybe they hadn't come to bump off Dave but for some other reason. It could be they'd come after Tex himself, that after Sam had lost whichever of them he'd heard outside Dave had gone out to explore and had surprised either the Doc or Poston, getting killed for his pains. It could be that way, but it was only guesswork.

'How 'bout the Kid?' asked Pop. 'Maybe he was still hangin' around last night. He ain't above lootin' a ranch, I guess, nor above killin'.'

Tex shrugged his shoulders. Pop might be right, but there were reasons against it. For one thing the Kid was experienced and wasn't likely to try breaking into a ranch-house with a couple of dozen cowhands in the bunkhouse right near. This same argument made him wonder whether the Doc and Poston would have risked getting after him himself, too. Another reason against the Kid theory was that it was known that the bandit always went for pretty big loot. The Bar X was run down, there wasn't much worth taking at the place. The Kid was sure to realize that. A third point was that a knife had been used, which wasn't the Kid's weapon.

Guys tended to stick to their chosen weapons, as Tex knew. The Kid had the reputation of fighting fair, using guns. Tex didn't reckon he'd killed Dave; the murder was linked with the Parson's set-up.

Getting back to the Doc and Poston, who if they'd had a hand in the killing had acted on the Parson's orders, that went without saying, it wasn't sure exactly when they'd done it. It seemed that Sam had left the house at about the time Tex himself was clearing from the hotel. If the murder had been committed pretty soon after Sam had left the Doc could have done it, but not later, for then he had been a long way down the trail. The same applied to the sheriff.

Why he'd retraced his steps later and come up trail again from the other direction, Tex couldn't know, nor why the Doc had turned off.

He reckoned it was time to reveal to Sam that he'd encountered Linda; and to Pop about the bloodstains.

'I ain't finished yet,' he said heavily. 'I met up with Linda Forbes. Pop knows that, but you don't Sam.'

Briefly he described the encounter. Sam stared at him.

'Heck, the dame . . . an' Buck was away from the Lazy Y, that's somethin' maybe you've forgotten?'

Tex hadn't forgotten it. But he still hadn't finished.

'She had blood on her shirt sleeve,' he stated flatly. 'She don't know I saw it. I guess I didn't talk about it. I didn't know then that Dave had handed in his checks.'

There was silence while this lot was digested. It was broken by Pop.

'It don't make sense,' he muttered. 'Linda ain't . . . heck, she ain't a killer.'

Sam's face was puckered. Then he spoke.

'Maybe she ain't, though she can use a gun OK. But maybe she knows a lot.'

He was voicing Tex's own thoughts. He didn't like them but he couldn't avoid them. Maybe the girl had picked up the stains innocently, but much as he wanted to believe this Tex couldn't. Coincidence was all right up to a point, but not beyond it.

'I guess we got to talk to the dame,' muttered Sam. 'If she knows anythin' she's got to talk.'

Tex nodded. Again Sam was voicing his thoughts, thoughts that had been with him all morning. There had got to be a show-down with Linda Forbes – but maybe not just yet. If she knew anything she wouldn't talk unless forced. Tex didn't see himself manhandling her nor allowing anyone else to do that. But maybe she'd give a lead if she was watched.

Pop Dwight changed the subject, reverting to something briefly discussed earlier.

'What you make o' the fifty-fifty splittin' o' the profits?' he asked abruptly.

Tex brought his attention back to Pop. He began to roll a cigarette.

'I guess maybe somethin' could be made o' that,' he replied. 'You think about it, Pop, an' I reckon you'll be able to work it out.'

Pop Dwight wrinkled his forehead, stuck out his underlip.

'You mean you reckon. . . ?'

He got no farther for through the closed window leading on to the verandah came the sound of approaching riders. Tex went swiftly to the window in time to see a bunch of guys sweep into view, with the sheriff in the lead, behind him Doc Black and Buck Forbes. Sam and Pop, joining Tex, recognized one or two other ranchers. This wasn't the Parson's usual bunch of hoodlums, then, though there were a few of his boys present, including Jeb, his foreman.

'What's the game?' muttered Sam, dropping his hand to his Colt. 'I reckon this don't look so good, Tex.'

'Pop, go an' find out,' said Tex, turning to the older man. 'I ain't bein' taken for another ride. If they're after me take your hat off, that'll give me the tip an' I'll vamoose. If it's OK keep your hands away from your hat.'

Pop nodded, opened the window and passed through. Tex watched closely as he approached the bunch, now drawn up and dismounting by the corral. Sam had slipped out the back to make sure Tex's pony was ready and waiting in case it was needed.

He saw Pop come up to the bunch and talk with Poston. He didn't raise his hands to his Stetson, kept them both stuck in his gun-belt. Then he turned and with Poston, Buck, Doc Black and Werner of the Block Diamond – from the description Sam and Pop had provided of the guy Tex could place him – came back to the living-room.

As they crowded in Sam slipped back into the room, giving Tex the signal that the pony was ready. It looked like it wouldn't be necessary, though. Pop was satisfied that there was no danger and Tex didn't want to vamoose unless it was necessary. There was a lot he wanted to know.

'The sheriff's got a lead,' said Pop. 'He reckons he's got proof Brady bumped off Dave. He's come to get him.'

Sam let fall an oath. Tex stared at Poston and then at Doc Black whose saturnine face was inscrutable. Tex didn't get there . . . but he did a moment later. The Doc's hand moved slickly to his rod and drew it. At the same time Poston, Buck, Jeb and Werner drew their own rods.

'OK, stick 'em up,' snapped Poston, jerking his gun at Tex, while the others covered Sam and Pop. 'I guess you fell for the baloney all right. We weren't takin' no risks with you, Scarron, seems like you're mighty fly.'

Tex put up his hands, there was nothing else for it. Tex had been foxed by the phoney tale about Brady, and before him Pop had been taken for a ride.

'OK, I guess there won't be no trouble now,' continued Poston. 'The boys outside'll look after the rest of the outfit. I'm arrestin' you, Scarron, for murder. Steel and you Pop, I guess had better come along for questionin'.'

Sam broke into speech. What the heck did Poston think he was talkin' about? Tex wasn't a murderer.

'He was down at the River when Dave was bumped off,' rasped Sam, 'He was talkin' with the Parson.'

Tex would have stopped him if he could, because even now he didn't want it known for sure that he'd aimed to bluff the Parson. If the Parson wasn't yet certain of that, which might be the case, time might be bought while he questioned Tex and checked up. Things weren't looking so good right now. The more time he could buy before the bunch tried lynching him again, this time for murder and this time, no doubt, with some apparently legal justification, the better. Time might be bought if the Parson wasn't dead sure about what Tex had aimed to do, how much he knew and how much he'd talked. But Sam had shot his mouth and when the Parson heard about that he'd know that Tex had been bluffing, otherwise he wouldn't have told Sam he'd been down at the hotel with the Parson.

But maybe it didn't matter, not if Brady had eavesdropped and already talked. The fact that Brady's name had been used to bluff was another, though minor indication that the guy was in with the Parson.

Buck Forbes broke in.

'You got a nerve,' he snarled. 'You reckon the Parson'll give this guy an alibi? He wasn't down at the River last night, the Parson has said he ain't seen him since he stacked the deck night before last. But I guess the Doc saw him.'

'Sure, he saw him, hangin' around up here,' broke in Poston. 'He saw him knife Brand . . . he'll give evidence and then I guess we'll string Scarron up.'

Pop wasn't standing for that. He could prove that Tex had ridden to the River, that he'd met up with him later and then Tex had tried to strike the Doc's trail.

'And you were hangin' around, Poston,' added Pop, 'we saw you . . . an' earlier you came down the trail from these parts.'

Poston drew back his lips.

'Reckon you know a mighty lot. Sure I was around, on official business, an' so was the Doc. He's been sworn in as a deputy. You ready to say you saw this guy Scarron reach the River? It don't signify, because I guess you won't be believed by the jury, brother. Scarron came back an' bumped off Brand . . . I reckon he wanted to lay hands on the ranch, we all know it's his now, Brand talked 'bout who he was leavin' it to. The Doc saw him knife the old guy but he couldn't do anythin' to stop him. He ought to have told me before what he saw, but seems like he was hopin' to get Scarron himself, only then he had the sense to change his mind and lay information.'

It was about the phoniest tale ever put up. The holes in it would have made a net . . . but that didn't signify, as Tex realized. This was a frame-up, a clumsy one, but it would serve its purpose. Justice in these isolated parts was dispensed by the sheriff. Sure there'd be a kind of court, with a jury, but that'd be packed. In the Phoenix court the charge wouldn't lie, but it would out here. The Parson would see to that; and maybe somebody else would take a hand, an unobtrusive hand. Tex hadn't forgotten the fifty per cent splitting of the Parson's careful accounts.

Tex hadn't reckoned on being grabbed again, but he'd had a fast one pulled on him. He hadn't expected a move of this sort – it was clever, no doubt about that. And maybe he wouldn't live to be tried. That was a possibility, in fact a probability. He reckoned Sam and Pop were for it by now, too. The Parson probably judged that Pop was in with him, would do when it was reported that Pop had tried to give him an alibi. Sam and Pop would be bumped as well.

The outlook wasn't all that hot.

CHAPTER 13

Once more Tex rode down the Bar X trail towards Grant's River – but not the way he'd meant to ride. His wrists were bound behind his back and he was closely guarded by armed men, his pony led by Jeb. Behind came Sam and Pop.

There wasn't a chance of making a break for it. And this time, Tex reckoned, his captors would take better care that he didn't get away. In all there were more than a dozen guys, all well armed and all on the alert. This was a sheriff's posse, carefully selected, Tex reckoned, to give an appearance of legality. He hadn't much doubt that the ranchers present, Werner of the Block Diamond, for example, and a guy he took to be Josh Malloney, of the Indian Range joint, had been brought along for that purpose.

The charge of murder was a clumsy frame-up, but it would serve the Parson's purpose. Clumsy all right because Doc Black had obviously only just been tipped off to fake his yarn that he'd seen Tex commit the murder. The Doc had been up to the Bar X during the morning with the sheriff but hadn't said a word then about what he was supposed to have seen. The reason given by Poston why the Doc hadn't talked before was so phoney nobody but a lunatic or a crook would believe it. The Parson wasn't a lunatic and neither were the other guys who would form the jury, but they were crooks or else bought. Tex knew he was for it, one way or another.

His mind was working quickly as he rode with the escort down the trail. Either there'd be a mock trial and then a hanging or else it'd be worked so that he was bumped off before then. The story would be that he'd tried to make a break for it. Sure, that was the likeliest. In any event the outlook was grim.

The Parson had brains all right. This was a neat way of getting rid of a guy who wasn't wanted, who was considered dangerous. It had been a neat way to grab him, too, of putting him off his guard. He'd been foxed, just the way the Parson had intended. Or maybe just the way somebody else had intended. That was a thought nibbling away at the back of Tex's mind . . . but it didn't look as though it mattered much now whether he was right or wrong over that. He had been in some tough spots before, but none tougher than this. This time there wouldn't be any playing at lynching, he reckoned. He was for it.

It meant that the Parson had rumbled him, knew that on the previous night he'd aimed to bluff him, knew that he was here to bust the rackets and was dangerous. Or again, somebody else knew all that. It didn't matter which . . . quite a lot was known by the enemy. Maybe it had been guesswork, but Tex didn't think so. If the guy Brady, whose name had been used to bait the trap at the Bar X, was in with the Parson, that would explain the knowledge possessed. It was possible, then, that the Parson had been warned in advance that Tex was aiming to get down to the hotel; but the fire, which he couldn't have known about, had maybe startled him into leaving the hotel. Or word that Tex was on the level, intending to bust open the rackets, might have reached the Parson after the hotel incident. It didn't make a lot of difference. The Parson now aimed to liquidate the guy he reckoned was dangerous.

The charge was a frame-up. But somebody had killed Dave. Like Snake earlier, Tex got that far without difficulty. It was long odds that the Parson's bunch were responsible for the killing; but again why? Dave had paid his dues, there didn't seem any reason for killing him off. An accident maybe? It could be, but Tex had a hunch it wasn't that way. Dave had been bumped off deliberately . . . for what motive?

Tex's thoughts were interrupted as a narrow defile was reached. It stretched for only a quarter of a mile, where the trail wound between two outcrops coming close together. The sheriff and Doc Black went first, guns out; behind them came Jeb leading Tex's beast and alongside Tex was Buck Forbes. Tex hadn't forgotten that Sam had discovered that Buck had been away from the Lazy Y on the previous night. And certainly he hadn't forgotten that Linda Forbes had acted mighty queer on more than one occasion.

Tex didn't have time to think any more about this, however. He was halfway through the defile, with Poston and Black well ahead, when without warning things began to happen. There was a sudden tremendous explosion coming from the River end of the defile, a roar that made the ear-drums sing, and the earth shook and heaved.

Tex was flung from the saddle. As he fell he saw and heard rocks splitting asunder, a chasm open miraculously in the trail a hundred yards ahead. Then a choking cloud of dust swept down the defile blotting out the afternoon sun.

There was chaos. Horses stamped and reared, screaming with terror. Men shouted, others called out in pain. Through the diminishing roar of the explosion and the clattering of rocks hurled down from the outcrops, could be heard the crack of six-shooters.

Tex tried to get to his feet, but Jeb's pony was lying half across him, hoofs thrashing. The huge Jeb himself could be glimpsed through the dust cloud lying on the ground; others, including Buck Forbes, had also been flung down.

Then through the dust came a man on foot. For the second time since reaching the Grant's River territory Tex was released by a swiftly flashing knife that severed the ropes at his wrists.

Then he was able to stagger to his feet. The defile was in wild confusion, a mass of plunging, panic-stricken ponies and men, some on foot, others still in the saddle but their beasts out of control, yet others lying on the trail. And helping Tex to his feet was a guy dressed all in black, a black kerchief round his face leaving only his eyes to be seen. The Kid had taken a hand again.

He thrust a Colt at Tex.

'Get goin',' he snapped, and thrust Tex away from him towards one side of the defile where there was a steep goat-track leading up the outcrop.

As he spoke Jeb hauled himself to his feet. The Kid's gun spoke and Jeb sank back again, though Tex couldn't see in the confusion and through the dust, still hanging over the defile, whether he'd been hit.

He didn't wait to find out. He made for the goat-track and nobody hindered him. The explosion, which had rent a great chasm across the defile at its River end, had created such chaos that nobody had time to spare except for his own welfare.

Tex came to the top of the outcrop and found the Kid close behind him.

'OK, brother, don't hang around, these guys'll come gunnin' for us,' rasped the bandit. 'You stick close to me.'

Tex wasn't having that. There was Sam to be thought about, and Pop Dwight. They'd been riding behind him, he hadn't seen them since the explosion. He wasn't clearing until he knew they were OK and free.

'They'll be OK,' was the swift reply. 'My buddy's lookin' after them, they weren't so near the fireworks, guess they're . . .'

He broke off, grabbed Tex's arm and swung him round. Away to the right, coming into sight from the end of the defile nearest to the Bar X, were three guys on horses. The dust, thick in the defile, didn't obscure the view on the top of the outcrop. Tex could recognize both Sam and Pop. With them was another, the sun shining on the black kerchief covering his face.

Tex didn't argue any more. From behind, from the defile, could still be heard the noise of horses and men in wild confusion. Tex could hear the crack of shots as well. The posse must be firing wildly, those that could get at their rods.

'OK, brother?' snapped the Kid.

'Sure . . . I'm comin'.'

The Kid moved on swiftly, Tex following. Tex now had a gun, but the Kid didn't seem to rate the chances very high that he'd use it on him. He led the way over the broken ground which stretched in a slope from the top of the outcrop, ground which afforded excellent cover. After some half a mile he came to a declivity where a couple of ponies were uneasily tethered. Obviously they hadn't liked the explosion even though they were tethered at some distance from the defile, but they were OK and under control.

'Guess we can move quicker on these,' grunted the Kid, and threw the reins of one of the beasts to Tex.

Tex grabbed them and mounted. There were a heck of a lot of things he wanted to know, but this wasn't the moment to start enquiring. The explosion, dynamite had been responsible, he guessed, had thrown the posse into confusion, but it couldn't be long before it sorted itself out. The advantage of numbers had been offset but that could only be temporarily. This was the moment to vamoose, and quick.

An hour later Tex was finding out much of what he wanted to know; and learning a whole lot he hadn't expected. The Kid had led him into the foothills and to a cave cut in the face of a cliff, a cave evidently used as a hideout. Sam and Pop, uninjured, were there when he arrived, and with them was the Kid's buddy. Sam and Pop had been snatched with less difficulty than Tex himself, for they had been farther away from the explosion and their beasts hadn't been so maddened.

By now the Kid and his buddy had discarded the kerchief masks. The Kid, Tex saw, obviously had Mexican blood; he was lean and dark, with a sharp thin face. His buddy wasn't Mexican or anything like it. Tex put him down as an Arizona guy or maybe from Colorado. He was broad and thick, with a rugged, weatherbeaten face.

The Kid had talked a bit. The rescue had been skilfully planned and contrived, dynamite being planted at the end of the defile and touched off at the moment when it would throw the posse into confusion but not inflict injury on the prisoners. That must have been pretty tricky to work out as Tex realized, dynamite being unpredictable stuff.

'Sure, but we managed,' said the Kid easily, speaking softly with just a trace of Mexican accent. 'We reckoned the trail was 'bout the only one they could bring you guys.'

Sam broke in violently. Why had the Kid gone to all that trouble to grab them, how had he known they were being taken to Grant's River?

'And heck, where'd you get the dynamite?' he added. 'I reckon we're grateful, but. . . .'

Pop Dwight interrupted, staring at the Kid.

'Sure, I reckon they're fair questions,' he said. 'And you ain't in the habit o' goin' around with your face uncovered, I guess. What's the game, Kid?'

Tex said nothing but waited for the Kid to answer. He did so as he skilfully rolled a thin, yellow cigarette. There had been no pursuit, or if there had been it had failed to pick up the trail. The Kid's buddy, whom he called Slick, which maybe wasn't such a bad name at that, was keeping the broken ground in front of the cliff under observation, but there wasn't any movement or glimpse of the Parson's bunch.

'We got the jam from the Lazy Y,' drawled the Kid. 'Sure, they been doin' some blastin' lately and the stuff was left over. It came in handy.'

'The Lazy Y!'

The Kid nodded but didn't look at Sam. He spoke directly to Tex.

'Sure, the dame brought it along. She knows what she's doin' I guess. A mighty pretty girl,' he added.

Tex stiffened. There wasn't any doubt the Kid was talking about Linda. Matters had gone 'way beyond Tex. He didn't know whether he was coming or going.

Before he could speak Slick jerked out some words over his shoulder.

'She's comin',' he said.

Tex swung round and stared out over the broken ground. After a bit he picked up a movement, and then saw Linda riding towards the cliff alone.

'I guess she'll do the talkin',' drawled the Kid at his elbow.

Tex said nothing for a few moments as he watched the girl approach. Then he did speak.

'I reckon maybe she tipped you off we were for it?'

'Sure, she tipped us off . . . but wait for it, brother. She'll do the explainin'.'

They waited, Tex and his buddies tensely, the Kid easily, drawing at his cigarette. Only once did he speak while they watched the girl approach the hideout.

'I've heard 'bout you, Scarron,' he said. 'Seems like you're a fair guy . . . the hombres you've laid for up north I ain't got no use for. I ain't got no use for the Parson, either, nor the guy who's behind him.'

Tex looked at him sharply then but had no chance to reply because Linda came up. She dismounted, aided by Slick, and then moved across to Tex and the others.

She didn't pay much attention to Sam or Pop, concentrated on Tex. For a moment nothing was said. Then Tex spoke.

'Seems like we got to thank you for quite a bit,' he said slowly. 'And it looks like I got you all wrong. What's the set-up?'

She dropped her eyes for a moment but then raised them again. A smile fluttered at her lips.

'I thought maybe you'd got me wrong. I didn't want that but I wasn't sure of you, especially when you pulled the one you were workin' in with the Parson. But then I found that was wrong and I reckoned we ought to work together – and with the Kid.'

Tex passed up some of the questions he wanted to ask in favour of one in particular.

'How'd you find out I wasn't in with the Parson?'

She shrugged her shoulders, after a swift glance at the Kid, a glance which Tex noticed.

'I get around,' she replied. 'I got word what the Parson was aimin' to do, grab you for the killin'. I reckoned you'd got to be snatched . . . it's like I said, you're after the Parson, and so are we . . . and the guy behind him.' She paused and then added, 'I guess you don't know nothin' 'bout that, though.'

Sam broke in hurriedly.

'What guy behind him?' he asked. 'You mean the Parson ain't boss o' the rackets?'

Linda Forbes looked across at the Kid again before replying.

'We reckon there's somebody in with him,' she said slowly. 'Maybe he's the boss, maybe he's only a partner, but there's somebody behind the Parson, somebody who keeps in the background. My guess is he's got more brains than the Parson.'

'Sure . . . an' the Parson splits fifty-fifty with him,' interrupted Tex. 'I got on to that. An' the mutual protection racket ain't the only one bein' worked. I reckon maybe Werner is bein' blackmailed, an' there's rustled cattle been sold.'

The Kid intervened then.

'You got the right idea, brother. I reckon we ought to start from the beginnin'. You ain't told the guy how you came to meet up with me,' he added, turning back to the girl.

'No, like you say, we'd better start from the beginnin'.'

The Kid left it to her. After a bit she started in talking, and went on for some time. Tex listened without interruption. Sam looked as though he wanted to break in every now and again but he held his horses. Linda did all the talking for some time.

It seemed the Kid had heard about the Parson operating his rackets in the River district; and he'd heard something else, too – that there was another guy in with the Parson, a guy keeping under cover. Linda didn't go into details of how the Kid had heard, and later on the Kid didn't amplify, either. Not that it mattered. The point was that some years before the Kid had been hi-jacked over some cattle, south of the Mexican border, by a guy who was then running a rustling racket.

'The Kid was swindled,' continued the girl, 'and the guy got away, beating him to it. A few weeks ago he got the tip this same guy might be in with the Parson. It linked up, because the Kid had heard earlier that the guy who'd hi-jacked him came from these parts. He came to have a look round.'

By accident Linda had fallen in with the Kid. He'd done her a good turn, when her pony had bolted, scared by a thunderstorm.

'He saved my life I reckon, stopped me goin' over the edge of Hunt's Dip . . . after that we got together. He was after the Parson and this other guy and so was I.' She paused and added, 'You see, Buck is bein' taken for a ride. He don't know I'm on to it, but he's bein' milked. He's mortgaged the ranch to the Parson now. I reckon it won't be long before the Parson forecloses.'

Tex was beginning to understand quite a lot. This dame was working in with the Kid, working with him and against the Parson – but making out she was unsuspicious of the Parson. Sure, that explained why she took a hand in the hills when Tex went after the Kid. It looked like the Kid had laid for Jeb and Snake, maybe to try and get some information out of them – and Linda knew about it.

There was something else, too. Tex remembered he'd shot his mouth about going after the Kid.

'You didn't want that, I reckon,' he said, when the girl came to an end of the first part of her story. 'So you aimed to get me run out o' town an' scared off?'

She faced him frankly.

'Yes, but I didn't know they were goin' to lynch you. You've got to believe that. I wanted you out of the way. We've got to break these rackets before Buck loses everythin' he's got. It's not only him I'm thinking about, but his mother. If the Lazy Y goes it will kill her.'

Sam grunted. He reckoned from what he'd seen that the Kid ought to be able to look after the Parson easy enough. The Kid, swallowing smoke, spoke up.

'Maybe, an' I guess it wouldn't be much loss. I don't hold with this mutual protection racket. Me an' Slick, we reckon we're above that kinda racket. But we got to get the guy behind the Parson, and we don't know who he is – not yet.'

Pop Dwight saw the point all right, even if Sam didn't. To liquidate the Parson wouldn't be enough. The other guy, supposing there was one, would still be dangerous, and he'd still have the Parson's boys to use. To break the Parson wouldn't break the rackets.

'That's workin' it out there is somebody behind the Parson,' added Pop. 'But I don't reckon that's proved.'

'I guess there's somebody,' was Tex's reaction to this. 'I had a look at the ledgers . . . the Parson is splittin' fifty-fifty with someone. That makes it sure he's got a partner.' He paused and then spoke to Linda again. 'How'd you get the blood on your shirt last night? An' what were you doin' up near the Bar X?'

She was startled, there was no doubt about that. She hadn't known he'd seen the bloodstains. But she answered pat and Tex believed what she had to say.

She'd been up near the Bar X coming back from rendezvousing with the Kid and Slick.

'Sure, that's right,' said the Kid.

'That was Dave's blood.' Her voice was low. 'I saw him lyin' and went to see what I could do, but he was dead. That was when I got the blood. Then Sam Steel came and I cleared . . . he didn't see me.'

Sam gave an exclamation.

'You was there? Heck, you must've moved mighty slick.'

She nodded. Dave was dead, she could do nothing for him. When she heard Sam coming, and later, from cover had seen him with Dave, her instinct had been to get away. She'd ridden round a bit and then had met Tex.

'It's the truth,' she added. 'I don't know who killed Dave, but it must have been one of the Parson''s bunch.'

Tex believed her, on both scores. She herself hadn't been implicated, he was dead sure of that – and mighty glad to be sure. He was as sure that one of the Parson's bunch had murdered Dave. He wanted that guy, and the man behind this set-up here in Grant's River. The Parson himself ought to be easy, but not the other guy, nobody knowing who he was.

There was a whole lot to be discussed yet, a whole lot to be discovered from Linda and the Kid, but Tex had made up his mind on one point. The Kid had saved his life once for sure, maybe twice. Tex wasn't aiming to lay for the Kid. He'd work in with him.

'Guess that's the way you want it?' he asked, still looking at the girl.

'Yes . . . there's no sense in workin' against each other.'

'Sure, I'd rather work in with you,' was Tex's reply. 'Seems like I owe you quite a bit.'

At that Linda dropped her eyes abruptly.

'I couldn't let them hang you . . . or maybe put you out some other way,' she said.

CHAPTER 14

'I don't know I like it. This guy's a hoodlum, it ain't any use tryin' to make out he ain't. I reckon we're bein' rushed into workin' in with him.'

Sam Steel sat hunched on a boulder outside the cave talking to Tex and Pop but mainly to Tex. Sam was making it pretty plain that now he was getting his bearings he wasn't all that happy about the latest developments.

Tex and Pop didn't say anything. Some time had elapsed since the rescue at the defile and the subsequent first talk at the hideout. It was now growing dusk, the shadows lengthening over the broken ground stretching towards Grant's River.

Since the first talk there had been more detailed discussion, to which Sam and Pop Dwight had listened mostly in silence. Now the Kid was talking to Linda and Slick was keeping watch, which left the other three to themselves.

Tex could understand something of how Sam felt – and maybe Pop, too, though the latter hadn't yet committed himself. Here they were promised to work in with the Kid and Slick against the Parson and whoever was behind him. That was OK as far as it went. The Kid was a guy who knew how to look after himself, and looked at one way he and his buddy were useful recruits. But that didn't overcome the fact that they were both bandits, wanted by the law.

Tex drew at his cigarette, thinking. During the talk that had followed the first show-down, Linda had revealed that there had been no killing at the defile. The dynamite charge had been set-off at exactly the right moment. Eventually the sheriff's bunch had sorted themselves out and had ridden back to the River, not attempting any pursuit which by then was obviously hopeless. Linda had been at the settlement waiting on events, having ridden there after contacting the Kid. She had brought word that none of the posse had been seriously injured. Jeb was OK which proved that the Kid's shot had missed him.

Buck Forbes was all right, too. Linda hadn't known that her cousin was to be with the posse, hadn't apparently worked out that he might be. She was glad he hadn't been hurt but she hadn't said much about that.

Tex was thinking about Buck right now. According to Linda he didn't know that she had found out that he'd mortgaged the Lazy Y to the Parson, presumably as security for the poker debts. The girl maintained that probably Buck thought this was just a formality. She'd tried to convince her cousin that the Parson was a crook, but Buck wasn't having any. When it suited him the Parson would foreclose. The fact that Buck didn't pay any protection dues proved to her that he was being kept happy for larger picking later.

Maybe this was all true, but Tex wasn't taking it necessarily at its face value. Buck Forbes had been out on the previous night. Linda didn't know that; when she was told she'd had no idea where he'd been. She herself, of course, had been out and thus unable to keep tabs on her cousin. The guy behind the Parson was clever, there was no doubt about that. He covered his tracks pretty well.

Tex was thinking about other points, too. The Kid, now . . . was he on the level, for the purpose of getting the Parson and the guy behind him? Was he on the level or bluffing? Had he, for example, killed old man Dave and now aimed to put the crime on the Parson. Tex didn't reckon so, couldn't see the point of the two rescues if the Kid was playing a crooked game. He'd rescued Tex from the lynching; then, as Tex now knew, not knowing that he had any connection with the Parson affair. He just hadn't aimed to stand by while a guy was lynched. OK, then that incident probably had no significance either way. But the defile affair was different. The Kid had known all about Tex then. If he was playing a crooked game why run the risk of staging a rescue?

Tex considered Sam's views but dismissed them. The Kid was a bandit, outside the law, but the way things had worked out there wasn't much alternative to working in with him. It wasn't the first time Tex Scarron had operated with an outlaw. He owed the Kid his life, so did Sam and Pop. On the whole Tex reckoned the Kid was OK. He reckoned, too, that he was on the level with them, which was a matter of more importance than Sam's qualms of conscience.

'I reckon you're talkin' hay-wire,' said Tex at last, turning back to the others. 'I ain't lettin' up on the Parson an' I reckon you ain't, Sam? OK, we'd be loco to turn up the chance of help from the Kid and his buddy. He's on the level, I reckon, an' we can use him, same as he can use us, for the same object. What do you think, Pop?'

Pop Dwight nodded. He'd had plenty of time now to think about the new set-up. It didn't look as though the Kid could get much out of this business except revenge, but guys were queer. The Kid was after the guy who'd hijacked him and that could be sufficient motive. And Linda was an attractive girl . . . maybe the Kid wasn't immune to feminine charms. Like Tex, Pop couldn't work out any reason why the Kid should be bluffing them. He'd come clean it seemed, very clean, taking a risk in snatching them from the sheriff's posse and another in bringing them to the hideout – though Pop had noticed that he and Slick kept their rods handy all the time.

Another point that influenced Pop, as he said now, was the fact that he was fond of Linda and reckoned she was dead on the level. She was a great girl the way she'd tipped off the Kid to snatch them.

'I reckon we got to work in with the Kid,' he said.

Sam grunted, changed his ground.

'OK, I guess you're right, but I ain't got no experience joinin' up with bandits.' Then, abruptly, 'How did Linda know what the Parson was aimin' to do?'

'Seems like there's somebody down at the River workin' in with her,' replied Pop slowly. 'But she ain't talkin' 'bout that an' neither is the Kid.'

This was true enough. Tex had picked up that point and pressed it a bit. Linda had discovered that the Parson aimed to grab them on a murder charge, him at all events, and maybe Sam and Pop as well. That was definite, but it hadn't been explained yet who had tipped her off. That was something yet to come.

'We got to get together an' work out the next move,' said Tex.

'The Kid told me he'd give me all the dope then. But Linda ain't stayin', she's gettin' back to the Lazy Y 'fore there's questions asked. Then I guess we'll get together with the Kid. He reckons he's got an idea how we can get the Parson and the other guy, but he ain't talkin' yet.'

He broke off as Linda came across.

'I'm goin' now,' she said. 'You hang around here with the Kid, I'll be up again tomorrow and maybe I'll have some more to tell you then. I reckon this is goin' to set the Parson back, losin' you the way he did.'

Tex reached for his Stetson.

'I'm going with you part o' the way,' he said. 'I ain't havin' you ridin' alone farther'n you need.'

He didn't much like her going back at all. She said she'd be safe enough and that nobody knew she'd tipped off the Kid or had any connection with him. Maybe that was right, but still Tex didn't like it. If she'd slipped up and the Parson suspected her he wouldn't pull any punches because she was a woman. But if she stayed at the hideout, didn't show up at the Lazy Y, that would maybe work out worse for her. There'd be a hue and cry with guys from the Lazy Y searching the hills. And her absence might well give the Parson the tip she wasn't what she seemed.

She looked at Tex askance.

'You reckon I can't look after myself?' she asked.

'I ain't takin' chances,' was the reply. 'Slick reckoned he saw a guy movin' around a while back. Let's go.'

It was true enough that Slick had thought he'd seen a movement half an hour earlier at a distance from the hideout. He'd gone scouting but hadn't come up with anyone. He admitted that maybe he'd been deceived by a shadow. But Tex wasn't taking any risks. There might be somebody hanging around. He was going to ride with Linda as near to the Lazy Y as he could get safely. The Kid, with Slick, Sam and Pop could look after themselves at the hideout for a bit.

Linda didn't raise any other objections and pretty soon she and Tex were riding away, using all the cover they could find. Darkness had come by now, and though the moon was up the light was poor, offering them good cover in itself. They rode silently, Tex going first, keeping to goat-tracks. Once away from the hideout the outcrops brooded silently. If there was anyone around then he was acting like a shadow. Tex reckoned the waste lands were deserted.

Without incident they came to within a mile of the Lazy Y, having seen nobody on the way. They had skirted the settlement, glimpsing the lights in the distance but keeping them well to the south. During the whole trip they hadn't spoken.

Now Linda drew up. In the far distance could be seen lights, those of the Lazy Y ranch-house.

'I'll be all right now,' said the girl, 'and you mustn't come any closer.' She paused and then added, 'Thanks for bringin' me, Tex.'

'That's OK.'

There was silence again. She made no attempt to break it but Tex was aware that she was glancing sidelong at him. At last he spoke again, abruptly.

'I reckon you've been mighty worried about Buck,' he said.

'Yes . . . don't get him wrong, Tex. Oh, I know he took the lead over that fake lynchin' and maybe you haven't got much to thank him for, but he's a good guy really, when you get to know him. He lost his father pretty young and he's had to make his own way since then. He's young . . . sure, I know he's older than I am, goin' by years, but . . . he's only a kid. He thinks he's smart but. . . .'

Her voice tailed away. Now she wasn't looking at Tex but staring ahead at the distant lights of the Lazy Y.

'You're pretty fond of him?'

Tex phrased it like a question but to him it wasn't really a question. He reckoned that Linda had proved she was fond of her cousin, the things she'd done to try and save him from himself. Tex had never met any girl like Linda Forbes. She was lovely to look at, essentially feminine, but she could use a gun like a man and she was tough, must be. She'd linked up with the Kid, all to break the Parson . . . not so much to break the Parson, Tex worked out, as to stop Buck ruining himself. Sure, she was fond of Buck.

'Of course I'm fond of him,' she replied, 'and of my aunt. I wish you could meet her, Tex.'

He said nothing. He reckoned he could work it all out for himself. There wasn't any reason why cousins shouldn't marry. Maybe that was the way it would work out. Maybe not, but Tex wasn't saying anything about that, nor about the possible reason why it wouldn't work out that way. He was thinking that the whole shoot served him right. This was the first time he'd ever looked twice at a girl. He'd decided a long time ago that game wouldn't pay off. Now he'd proved it – the hard way. It served him right.

She spoke again, still sitting her pony, making no attempt to clear.

'Buck has somethin' to thank you for,' she said, 'only he doesn't know it, I suppose. You saved him losin' more dollars to Spike, didn't you?'

He shrugged his shoulders. This was the first time the poker incident at the hotel had been mentioned since they'd met in the foothills after Dave's murder.

'I stacked the deck,' he said, 'but not usin' two aces. It didn't get me far, though. I guess you've picked up with some queer hombres,' he added. 'There's the Kid and there's me . . . I know most o' the tricks. But I'm on the level.'

He didn't quite know why he emphasized this. It should be obvious by now that he was on the level; and it couldn't matter to him anyway what she thought of him. But something made him speak that way.

She turned to him impulsively.

'I know that, Tex. Thanks . . . for bringin' me this far, I mean. I'll be seein' you.'

She touched her pony and the beast moved. But as it did so it caught its forefoot in a hole and stumbled. The girl would have fallen, taken unawares, but Tex was there and caught her.

For a moment she was in his arms, her slim, firm body close to his. She felt his arm round her, looked up and caught a glimpse of something in his eyes that brought a hot surge of colour to her face. It was only for a moment that she lay in his arms, but it was enough. Linda knew then something which it was no longer necessary for Tex to tell her.

She drew herself away from him.

'It's all right . . . thank you.'

With that she jerked the reins and was away, this time without incident. Tex sat his beast and watched her go, watched until she was out of sight round a bend in the track. He could still feel her body in his arms.

Then he turned his pony and made back up the track, striking towards the hills and the hideout which he had left with Linda more than an hour before. He'd ridden to Grant's River in the first place expecting trouble. He had found more than he'd anticipated; and now he'd found something else he hadn't banked on.

He rode for a long way without incident. Once more he skirted the settlement by some two miles, crossed the Bar X trail not far from the defile and so came to the broken ground running up to the hills. The territory seemed deserted. He reckoned that the Parson was probably down at the hotel mighty mad that his scheme had gone astray and that the guy he'd intended to liquidate had got away with it again. He wouldn't be so pleased either that the notorious Kid had taken a hand. Linda hadn't been able to find out how much the Parson knew about the affair at the defile, whether he knew that the Kid had been implicated, but it was good odds that he did know. The Parson wouldn't be so pleased.

Tex was anxious to reach the hideout and get down to it again with the Kid. He was a slick guy all right, must be after his lengthy experience. He reckoned he'd worked out how to break the Parson and get the guy behind him. Tex wanted to know what he'd got in mind.

He pushed on under the moon, which was fitful, passing now and again behind clouds. He came within half a mile of the hideout and then the silence which hitherto had brooded over the wastes was broken by the crack of a gun. Almost simultaneously there came other shots, a volley of them, from ahead of Tex, from the direction of the hideout.

Tex reined in as the shots cracked out and the flashes of flame seared the darkness. The cliff where the cave was situated reared up against the skyline clearly to be seen, for though the moon had gone behind clouds the sky was fairly light. There wasn't any doubt that the shots had come from the hideout or very near to it. As Tex reined in, grabbing for his Colt, he was remembering the movement Slick had glimpsed in the distance more than two hours earlier. There was trouble broken out at the cave; maybe the hideout had been rumbled and word taken back to the Parson.

This was as far as Tex's thoughts took him, for from slightly behind him another shot spurted. The bullet flaked a chip from a boulder a couple of feet to his right. Then he was out of the saddle and on the ground. Another shot cracked. He pin-pointed the direction from the stab of flame and fired back. He had walked into trouble himself. The area here must be swarming with guys. It didn't take much working out whose guys.

He fired again into the gloom but didn't know whether he scored a hit. He found cover behind a rock by the side of the track he had been following, but even as he did so he was attacked from the flank, where he was not covered by the rock. There was the crack of a shot and his Colt spun from his hand. He was unwounded but the bullet had struck the gun.

He grabbed for his other Colt but before he could draw it there was a rush from behind. He swung round but too late. He glimpsed a figure, shadowy but huge, and then the butt of a gun crashed down across his skull.

CHAPTER 15

The Parson was in his office at the hotel, smoking and thinking. It was the next afternoon and he had plenty to think about; considering everything he was more at ease than he might have been. Things had worked out well enough, much better than they might have done. When the Parson had received word that Tex Scarron, Sam and Pop had got away in the defile, and furthermore had been snatched by a guy pretty certainly identified as the Kid, it had looked bad.

He'd wanted Scarron out of the way, for he knew a dangerous guy when he saw one. He'd had his plans nicely laid, these including other items besides the liquidation of Tex. With that guy out of the way and put where he couldn't do any harm or interfere with future operations, the Parson would have been sitting pretty. After that he'd get the guy he'd been forced to split the profits with. There was another move he had in mind, too, which could come when he'd settled up the other business. There was the Lazy Y, a ranch that could be made to show a good profit once the Parson got his hands on it.

All that could be made to come about, but first the Parson needed Tex Scarron out of the way. He wasn't making any move in his intricate plan of operations until the newcomer was put where he couldn't do any damage. The Parson liked to make one move at a time.

Things had looked pretty bad, but now, only twenty-four hours after the affair at the defile, matters had worked out in a way the Parson wouldn't have believed possible. The break had come when word had reached the River that the fugitives were up at the hideout in the foothills and with them the Kid himself, his buddy . . . and Linda Forbes. The Parson hadn't wasted any time. He'd moved fast with a picked bunch of his boys. Right now he could relax. He'd got everything pretty well under control. Tex Scarron wouldn't be bothering him much longer and neither would the Kid.

He was aiming to work fast now. He didn't reckon he could miss getting to the position he'd planned earlier, before the rescue at the defile. There had been a bad slip-up over that but matters had righted themselves.

His thoughts were interrupted by a knock at the door. It was Buck Forbes, looking pretty worried. He came to the point quickly.

'You ain't seen Linda?' he asked. 'I been out lookin' for her. She cleared durin' the night and nobody ain't seen her since.'

The Parson's face remained impassive, though in fact he'd known for some time that the dame was missing from the Lazy Y. When he'd learned that she wasn't at the hideout in the hills he'd sent down to the Lazy Y. She'd been missing then. Buck wasn't the only guy who'd been searching for her, but the Parson wasn't giving anything away. He knew Linda Forbes had been playing a double game, but he wasn't talking.

'You don't want to get het-up, Buck,' he said easily. 'She gets around, always has done. She'll be OK.'

Buck wasn't to be fobbed off, though. He'd been out all day looking for Linda and hadn't found her. He knew that there had been action up in the hills on the previous night and he was worried.

'What about those guys you took?' he demanded. 'Maybe she got mixed up with 'em. I tell you I don't like it, Parson.'

The Parson himself wanted Linda Forbes, now that he knew she had been up at the hideout with Tex and the Kid. But he hadn't got her . . . maybe by now Jeb and Snake, out looking for her, had been lucky, but maybe not. The Parson wanted Linda, wanted to find out how much she knew.

'She didn't get mixed up with those hoodlums,' he replied. 'Take it easy, Buck, she knows how to look after herself.'

Buck, standing by the window facing Main Street, swung round.

'What about the guys you grabbed?' he asked. 'What do they know 'bout Linda?'

'Nothin' . . . and 'fore long they won't be knowin' anythin' 'bout anythin'. We got the Kid an' his buddy, an' we got Tex Scarron. We took him 'long with the Kid an' that's good enough. He'll swing an' so will the others.'

'You goin' to try 'em? When, Parson?'

'Tomorrow, I guess . . . they'll swing all right.'

Buck scowled, still thinking about Linda.

'I guess I want to talk to those hombres,' he growled. 'I ain't satisfied they don't know anythin' 'bout Linda.' And then, 'what 'bout the other two, Pop Dwight an' Sam? You didn't grab them?'

The Parson shook his head. No, they'd missed both Pop and Sam Steel. The guys hadn't been at the hideout when the attack was launched. Neither had Tex, but he'd shown up again at the right moment and Jeb had got him. Right now he was in the lock-up behind Main Street along with the Kid and the guy called Slick.

'We ain't got Sam or Pop,' the Parson corroborated, 'but don't let that worry you. They don't count for much ... I guess maybe they were workin' in with the Kid, but they ain't important. Maybe we'll grab them, but if not an' they clear that'll be OK. We shan't be bothered with 'em any more at the River.'

It was glib talk but the Parson wasn't as happy about the two guys as he made out. It was a pity they'd not been at the hideout when the attack was launched. Some of the boys were out looking for them, too. The Parson wished he'd laid hands on Sam and Pop – and on Linda – but he wasn't giving it away.

'I reckon we got the guy who bumped off old man Brand,' he continued. 'I guess I don't rightly know which of 'em it was, maybe it was Scarron or maybe it was the Kid himself, but it don't signify. They'll get a trial tomorrow and I reckon they'll swing. That'll look after whichever it was who knifed Brand.'

They'd all be looked after all right, but not the way the Parson was letting Buck believe. There wasn't going to be any trial; there was going to be an accident instead. But Buck didn't know that and wasn't going to know it.

The Parson went on talking, soothing him about Linda. It was well-known that the dame often went around on her own. She could look after herself ... there was nothing for Buck to worry about. Gradually Buck relaxed. He had always been easily influenced, especially by the Parson.

As for the Parson himself, while he was talking his mind was moving, but along different lines. As earlier when he'd first heard that the Kid was rustling in on the territory and he had persuaded himself that it didn't signify, so he tended to bluff himself that it didn't matter so much that Sam, Pop and the dame had escaped the trap of the previous night. It didn't matter, it would work out OK so he'd told himself. But now that Buck had brought up the subject again, the Parson was having second thoughts. It could be that the escapes would upset his plans.

While he talked to Buck he was indulging in these second thoughts. And all the time his eyes were on Main Street, hoping to get a sight of Jeb or Snake, maybe of Poston or the other boys, riding in with prisoners. He'd feel easier then.

They didn't come. The Parson took hold of himself. It was a bad habit of his to start doubting. Everything would be all right; it had got to be. He was expecting results too quickly, maybe.

Buck changed the subject of the talk. He had relaxed a bit by now, had stopped thinking about Linda.

'Parson, I guess I got to ask you somethin',' he said. 'It's been on my mind a bit . . . you ain't goin' to do nothin' with that mortgage?'

The Parson hadn't expected this but automatically answered smoothly, stringing Buck along as he had been doing for a long time.

'Don't worry 'bout that. Sure I hold the mortgage on the Lazy Y, but it's like I told you, it's a formality, that's all. I ain't thinkin o' fore-closin' if that's what you're worryin' about. You'll get enough dough back sometime to pay it off, Buck.'

Buck looked relieved.

'OK Parson, that puts it straight. Guess I was loco to worry. I'll be goin' . . . maybe Linda'll be up at the ranch when I get back.'

'Sure she will. You get along.'

Buck went and hadn't been gone above a few minutes before Snake rode into the settlement alone. He tethered his pony at the rail outside the hotel and sought the Parson.

He had nothing definite to report. He and Jeb had separated during the search for Linda. Snake himself had drawn a blank – and he hadn't seen either Sam or Pop Dwight.

'There ain't a chance up there, boss,' he said. 'I guess guys who don't want to be found ain't found in the hills. The same applies to the dame. I reckoned I ought to get along back. How's it goin'? You bumped off those guys yet?'

The Parson stubbed out his cigar.

'Not yet,' he replied briefly.

'Well, ain't you goin' to? I guess I don't fall for the tale you're goin' to try 'em, you ain't that slow.'

The Parson said nothing. Snake was right, he wasn't that slow. But the guy's arrival had brought to the forefront another problem, in the solution of which Snake had to take a leading part. The Parson was working things out.

As though reading his thoughts Snake spoke again, watching the Parson closely.

'You thought 'bout what we were talkin' 'bout?' he asked. 'I guess I'm ready when you are.'

Then the Parson broke his silence.

'Sure, I been workin' it out,' he said. 'I guess pretty near any time now. You hang around, Snake, don't leave the hotel until I tell you to . . . and keep your knife handy. I don't want no shootin'. You can use a knife OK?'

'I can use a knife. But I don't know who the guy is.'

Still the Parson wasn't to be drawn on the subject of identity. He wasn't taking any chances. If the projected killing didn't come off he didn't want Snake to know who his partner was . . . that might be dangerous. He'd give Snake the word at the last moment, not before. The Parson was a careful guy.

'OK, like you say, boss, I'll be around when you want me. You expectin' him down here?'

The Parson nodded. He reckoned he'd come – he'd have to make sure the prisoners were being taken care of and that plans to liquidate them were going forward OK. Sure, the guy would come . . . so the Parson hoped.

Snake rolled himself a cigarette, lit it before speaking again.

'You got slick word the Kid and this guy Scarron were up in the hills,' he drawled.

The Parson looked at him sharply for a moment and then away again.

'Sure, I got word . . . there was a guy hangin' around up there, doin' a bit o' trailin'. He sighted the bunch and got down here pronto.'

Snake nodded, sucked in acrid tobacco smoke.

'You ain't got around to dealin' with the black bum yet? Sure, I guess she'll keep.'

The Parson had pretty well forgotten about the grotesque Bluebell. She hadn't made any more trouble since the incident at the hotel, and neither had the Parson. It was like Snake said, she'd keep. When the other, major matters had been dealt with she could be looked after.

Those major matters would be looked after with any luck. First the three prisoners would be dealt with, or at least preparations made to that end. Then the Parson's partner could be liquidated; or maybe that would have to be attended to first, according to when he showed up. It didn't make much difference. Scarron, the Kid and his buddy were safe, couldn't get away, the Parson had made sure of that. It might work out that the guy Snake was to put out would get down to the settlement before the time came to liquidate the prisoners. If so then he could be put out first. If not then afterwards – it didn't really signify.

'How you goin' to work it for those guys?' asked Snake, jerking his head towards the rear of the hotel, where the lock-up was situated.

'I guess there'll be a fire,' said the Parson slowly. 'Too bad ... those guys tryin' to break out by firin' the place. Scarron knows all about oil,' he added, 'he's used it before, on my property.'

Snake allowed himself what he called a smile. Sure, a fire would settle the problem nice and easy. The sheriff would swear blind that it had been as a result of the prisoners trying to get away. After that Snake would use his knife, and maybe the Parson would frame that so it looked like Scarron or the Kid had bumped off the guy. Snake reckoned that could be worked, seeing that Poston was on the Parson's pay-roll. That would tidy things up nice and neat.

'Sure, that's about it,' agreed the Parson, who was prepared to go quite a long way with Snake, only holding back what could be dangerous for Snake to know. One of those items, apart from the identity of the Parson's partner, was that Snake himself wouldn't live long after the killing. Snake was going to be framed for the murder – though strictly speaking it wouldn't be a frame-up seeing that he was in fact going to do the killing. After that everything would indeed be tidied up, and the Parson would be sitting very pretty, in sole control.

'I guess you an' me can work in together OK.' drawled Snake. He had plenty of confidence now. 'You'll be foreclosin' on the Lazy Y, I reckon . . . and there's good pickin's from Werner, ain't there?'

'What you talkin' about?'

Snake's rat face creased into the travesty of a smile.

'It ain't no good bluffin', Parson . . . you don't want to try bluffin' a buddy. You an' me we're buddies now. I told you, I get to know things. You've been blackmailin' Werner, and I guess you ain't holdin' the mortgage on the Lazy Y just for fun.'

The Parson thought quickly. Snake knew more than he'd anticipated; but it was like he said, it was no use bluffing. No use and there was no need to bluff, because Snake wouldn't be alive long enough to make use of his knowledge.

'You're a smart guy, Snake . . . sure, you got it right. I've been stringin' Buck along, I'll grab the Lazy Y as soon as we've got the rest o' this settled. You'll get your cut, Snake.'

'Sure, I'll get my cut,' he replied. And then, 'Things have worked out all right, I guess. You an' me know Scarron didn't bump off old man Brand, an' neither did the Kid or his buddy, but it'll look that way if any questions get asked.'

'Sure . . . but I reckon you couldn't prove they didn't bump off Brand. Even you ain't so clever as that, Snake.'

Snake hitched up his gun-belt.

'Who did the killin'?' he asked. 'I reckon I'd like to know that . . . and I ain't got around to workin' out why, Parson.'

'You ain't got no interest in that, Snake . . . I guess it ain't your business. You use your knife when I tell you an' after that maybe we'll talk again.'

Snake was about to speak again when there came an interruption which took both the Parson and Snake off guard. The office door was flung open abruptly and there was a guy standing there with a gun in his hand, a guy who advanced into the room, the rod levelled, finger on the trigger.

It was Buck Forbes, his mouth set the way the Parson had never seen it before.

'Get your hands up,' he rasped, 'an' make it quick . . . my finger's itchin'.'

He was obeyed. There was death in his face, which both the others recognized.

The Parson found his voice first, even as he worked out how long he'd got to stall to make sure this mad guy was taken care of. The hotel was pretty well denuded of his boys because they were out looking for the other fugitives. That was why Buck had managed to pull a fast one. But there were some of the bunch hanging around.

'Cut it out Buck, this ain't no time for jokin',' said the Parson.

'This ain't no joke. You didn't shut the door on,' added Buck, jerking out the words at Snake. 'I been listenin' . . . I guess you can't bluff me any more, Parson. You're goin' to foreclose on the Lazy Y, an' you're aimin' to frame guys for a murder you know they didn't do. That's what you're aimin' to do, Parson, but it won't work out like that. I ain't standin' for that . . . I been a fool, I guess, but I've woke up now.'

The Parson's mouth set hard. So this dumb guy had been doing some overhearing. He'd got to be put out of the way.

'You got it all wrong, Buck,' he stalled, and then his eyes went beyond Buck to the half-open door. 'OK, Jeb,' he called, 'get him. . . .'

The bluff worked just long enough for the Parson's purpose. Buck half turned, as he did so the Parson moved. There was no Jeb in the doorway but that didn't matter. As Buck swung round again his gun was grabbed. The Parson knew his stuff, and there was Snake to lend a hand. Within a couple of seconds Buck was disarmed and looking at the wrong end of his own gun.

'I guess it's curtains for you, Buck,' snarled the Parson. 'It don't pay tryin' to pull a fast one on me. Sure, it's curtains . . . an' the Lazy Y will come to me OK on that mortgage I hold.'

Then somebody did show up in the doorway. It was Sheriff Poston. He wasn't alone. With him was Jeb . . . and Linda Forbes, held by Jeb, forced into the room.

'OK, boss, I got her,' grunted Jeb. 'I brought her in the back way, nobody didn't see me. . . .'

He broke off as his slow perceptions caught up with the fact that Buck was being held up.

'Heck, what the. . . ?'

'Cut it out, Jeb,' interrupted the Parson. Things were working out. The girl was taken, which was good, and the tables had been turned on Buck, which in view of what he'd heard was even better.

The Parson surveyed Linda, who stood there breathing hard, clothes dishevelled, shirt torn at the neck. Her face was white as she returned the Parson's gaze.

'Let her go, Jeb,' said the Parson smoothly. 'We got plenty o' guns . . . an' I reckon if anyone is goin' to handle this dame it'll be me. She ain't such a bad dish at that.'

Linda knew fear then, stark fear, for almost the first time in her life. When reluctantly Jeb released her one hand went to the neck of her shirt, pulling together the torn fabric from under which white flesh had shown.

The Parson laughed.

'I guess you needn't bother doin' that,' he said smoothly.

CHAPTER 16

Tex sat on the wooden floor of the lock-up situated behind the hotel and the sheriff's place next-door. Tex's ankles and wrists were tightly bound, too tightly either for comfort or any chance of escape. The Kid and Slick had been served in the same way.

All three had been prisoners in the lock-up for twenty-four hours. It was now dark; ever since the previous night they had languished in the lock-up, not knowing what was going on outside, what the Parson was doing – but able to make a pretty good guess what he intended. And Tex for one reckoned that he wouldn't delay much longer.

They knew, too, what had happened at the hideout and how the

Parson and his bunch had come to discover the place. They had been rumbled as a result of information reaching the Parson, there was no doubt about that. The Kid and Slick had talked – there had been plenty of time – and it seemed they'd sighted the hoodlums making straight for the hideout. The movement Slick had seen earlier had after all been significant. It had been some guy snooping around; and according to the Kid, who had been in better shape than Tex by the time the attack was over and the prisoners taken, it had been the Bar X cowhand Brady who had taken word to the Parson that fugitives from the defile affair were lying up in the hills. The Kid had heard the Parson say as much.

Tex had ridden into trouble and hadn't known anything for a long time after he'd been laid out. But he knew all about it now. He knew that Sam and Pop hadn't been taken at the hideout – and that was about the only cheerful piece of news there was. They had left the hideout soon after Tex himself had ridden away with Linda. They had gone to scout around. They hadn't returned by the time the attack was launched; as far as the prisoners knew they hadn't been taken yet. There was hope in this, pretty faint maybe considering how many hoodlums the Parson could command, but nevertheless a hope. Pop Dwight was past his prime but Tex knew that he was slick enough. Sam was young and tough. Sure there was hope that they'd do something.

The Kid and Slick, surprised and outnumbered by the Parson's bunch, had put up a fight but had been overwhelmed by weight of numbers. They hadn't been wounded but over-powered, had been made prisoners, along with Tex, and brought back to the River and locked up.

The hours passed slowly. They could talk but they couldn't move. Some food had been brought to them and water; they were left to eat and drink as best they could, still bound.

As to the outcome, there wasn't much doubt about that. The Parson must be aiming to liquidate his prisoners. Tex didn't reckon it would be done legally or even with a semblance of legality. The Parson wouldn't risk anything at this stage. In the first place Tex had judged that probably a swift killing would be staged with the excuse that the shooting had been done in self-defence or to prevent an arrested man escaping. Now he reckoned that the Parson would stick to that idea. An accident maybe would be staged, murder under the guise of misadventure. And time was moving relentlessly on, with no indication that Sam or Pop had managed to pull anything.

Any idea of making a break had long ago been discarded. The lock-up was of stout timber, with a single tiny window set high in one wall and heavily barred. Even if the prisoners could escape from the ropes which bound them there wouldn't be a chance of getting out of the lock-up. The doors were of solid oak equipped on the outside with a stout lock and iron bolts. But in any event it was impossible to shift the ropes.

Over and above his own personal jam, Tex Scarron was worrying about someone else – Linda. She had gone to the Lazy Y, but what then? The hideout had been rumbled by the guy Brady, there didn't seem any doubt about that. He had taken word to the Parson and the attack had been mounted. What else had he reported? Had he seen Linda up there with the others? It was possible, even probable. In that case the Parson would know that the girl was against him. Had he taken her by now?

Tex wasn't arguing with himself about Linda Forbes any more. He'd known her for about three days, and in that time had seen her only a few times, talked with her less. But Tex knew what he knew and at last admitted it freely. In the past he'd laughed at other guys who'd fallen for skirts, but right now he wasn't laughing. The thought of Linda in the Parson's power brought a fear that he had never known before, that he could never know on his own account. She was out of the common run all right, not only as to looks but also in being able to look after herself. But she'd be helpless against the Parson if and when he really got moving. Tex sat hunched against the wooden wall cursing himself. When Slick had reported the movement up in the foothills he ought to have gone after the guy, not been fobbed off with a tale that maybe it wasn't anyone. It had been someone all right and the guy, Brady probably, must have been closer to the hideout earlier, got a good look at those there. Tex didn't rate the chances very high that the Parson still didn't know that Linda was in the set-up against him.

The lock-up was dark, only a faint glimmer of light coming through the tiny barred window. Tex's instinct told him that the Parson had probably been waiting for nightfall. Now night had come. It could be that the prisoners had very little time left. Just what the enemy would pull Tex didn't know, but the main idea must be to liquidate those in the lock-up.

There had been silence for some time; there was little left to be said. But now the Kid's voice was heard.

'Somebody comin'.'

His ears were keen, far keener even than Tex's. The latter strained to listen; and then after a few moments he heard the noise that the Kid had picked up. There was a faint shuffling noise from outside.

Nobody said anything but it was odds that the Kid and Slick were thinking the same as Tex. The faint shuffling noise was furtive, which didn't look like the Parson or any of his boys were coming. They'd no reason to move cautiously. All three prisoners waited tensely.

The noise ceased, there was silence again. After a bit Slick started to speak.

'I reckon it ain't . . .'

'Cut it out,' came the Kid's order, 'Stay quiet, Slick.'

His buddy relapsed into silence again. Once more there was a tense pause. It lasted perhaps three minutes. Then at the door there came a noise again, a metallic noise, followed by the scraping of what could only be bolts.

The door opened though not fully. Tex had a glimpse of the sky outside and then it was blocked out by something that moved. Somebody had entered the lock-up . . . closed the door again, silently.

In the darkness Tex couldn't see who the guy was, had caught only a vague glimpse of somebody framed for a moment against the sky. But now he could hear whoever it was moving across the floor. Then a voice spoke softly . . . and Tex knew then that it wasn't a guy.

'Kid, you there?'

The intonation, the accent, were unmistakable. Tex had seen the grotesque negress Bluebell only once, hadn't ever heard her speak, but it was a negress who was now talking and it must be Bluebell.

'Sure . . . make it quick, honey.' Then, to Tex, 'I guess you didn't know 'bout Bluebell, Scarron. I kept quiet, reckoned I had to in case anyone was listenin' in. She's a pal o' mine.'

'Ah sure reckon Ah am,' came Bluebell's voice. 'Hold still, Kid, Ah'll have you out o' this. Ah been a mighty long time Ah know, but it weren't so easy grabbin' a key.'

Tex strained his eyes through the darkness but could see only vague movement on the other side of the lock-up. Bluebell was the Kid's buddy . . . that was a fast one. But it looked as though it was going to get them all out of a jam.

The Kid was released, then Slick, and lastly Tex. It took a little while for the circulation to get working again, for cramped limbs to return to normal. While they massaged wrists and ankles, Bluebell talked in a low voice, after getting across to the door again and making sure that nobody was hanging around.

She'd been working out how to get at the prisoners ever since they had been brought back to the River. It hadn't been easy and it had taken her all this time to manage it. But she'd worked it in the end.

'Sure, Ah lifted the key off the sheriff,' she added, 'an' Ah reckon he ain't got no idea, not yet.'

Then, as she drew from her capacious belt three guns, handing them out, she added something that brought Tex urgently to her side. Three hours earlier there had been a show-down between the Parson and Buck Forbes. Bluebell didn't rightly know what about, but her hunch was that Buck had at last got on to what the Parson was.

'An' not 'fore it was time, Ah reckon. The Parson was too quick for him . . . he's got him tied up in the hotel. And the dame's with him . . . Jeb got her up in the hills.'

Tex grabbed her by her huge arm.

'He's got Linda?' he rasped.

'Sure, but that ain't our worry, Ah guess. You guys got to scram . . .

an' maybe Ah'll come with you, Kid? Ah reckon Ah've had enough o' runnin' a store.'

Dimly Tex realized that the Kid must have planted Bluebell at the River deliberately, going to the trouble of buying out the guy Graw, presumably after he'd met up with Linda and agreed to lay for the Parson. But that didn't matter right now; nothing mattered except that Linda had been taken by the Parson. The Kid and his buddies could make a break for it if they liked, but Tex wasn't getting out without Linda.

'I'm stayin' until I've got her,' he said grimly. 'You'd better scram, Kid . . . an' thanks for what you've done, you an' Slick an' Bluebell.'

The Kid spoke briefly.

'It's OK, we ain't goin' just yet. I guess I wouldn't sleep comfortable knowin' that louse Dean had got the dame.' He turned to Bluebell. 'Where's the rat got her?'

Five minutes later the four of them were outside the lock-up, well under cover behind the hotel. It had been reckoned, evidently, that the lock-up was so secure that no guards were needed. As yet nobody knew that the prisoners were free – but it wouldn't be long before they did know.

Linda was in the room behind that which had witnessed the poker incident on Tex's arrival at Grant's River. This gave on to the waste ground behind Main Street. It was equipped with a window but according to Bluebell, Linda was well guarded, and with her Buck Forbes. What the Parson intended the negress didn't know, but at least when she had opened up the lock-up the girl had been in that room.

There was a light showing through the window, which was curtained, however, so that it was impossible to see into the room. Naphtha light spilled out from the front of the hotel on to Main Street as usual at this time, and there could be heard the usual noise from the saloon which by now must be pretty full. Where the Parson himself was there was no telling, but probably in his office. How many of his boys were with Linda or guarding the room from outside wasn't known either.

Not that it signified, because if there had been a hundred guys Tex was going in after Linda. There was neither time nor opportunity for finesse. The rescue must be launched swiftly and the chance taken that the surprise would pull it off. The Kid and Slick were tough and experienced. Tex reckoned without being told that Bluebell was that way, too. That made four of them, maybe against fifty . . . but surprise might offset the disparity in numbers.

They'd got it worked out as well as they could. In the front of the hotel, tethered to the rail, was a line of ponies. When the getaway was made, if it was made, some of these beasts could be used.

The Kid looked across at Tex as they crouched under cover only twenty yards from the rear of the hotel.

'OK, pal?'

'Sure, get goin' . . . an' good luck, Kid.'

The Kid smiled thinly. He reckoned they'd all need plenty of luck.

'When you get the dame, beat it,' he said, 'don't hang around. You know where to make for?'

Tex knew. The Kid had described another hideout in the foothills, at a distance from the first. If the party got split up, as was likely, they were all to make for this hideout which it was impossible for the Parson to know anything about.

The Kid got moving, and with him Slick and Bluebell. They slid from cover and made for the hotel, leaving Tex behind temporarily. Their task was to cause a diversion.

Slick and Bluebell made down the alleys on either side of the building, alleys which debouched into Main Street, one on either side. The Kid himself approached the rear entrance to the hotel.

Tex waited, watched Bluebell and Slick disappear and then the Kid enter through the rear door. Then he moved, leaving cover and sliding across the intervening space to the window of the room where it was to be hoped Linda was still a prisoner.

Tex reached the window, pressed himself against the wooden wall to one side of it. Within a couple of minutes there came a shot from the front of the hotel and it was instantly followed by uproar, with which were mingled other spasmodic shots.

It was time to act, and Tex didn't wait any longer. He heard the slam of a door near at hand, judged that it was the door of the room in which he was supremely interested. The window came pretty low, enabling him to set his shoulder against the glass and the frame.

His shoulder crashed through the glass and the flimsy wood and then lithely he was across the sill, flinging the curtains aside.

For a brief second he took in the scene . . . there was Jeb, in the act of swinging round, gun in hand, another of the Parson's bunch, Rocky Schultz, by the half-open door . . . and against the opposite wall Buck Forbes and Linda, both disarmed but neither of them bound. Just for a brief second Tex took this in and then his gun cracked as Jeb swung round. The man staggered back, blood welling from his shoulder. His gun fell to the ground. Then Rocky Schultz grabbed for his throwing knife. Tex fired again but too late. The sliver of steel hurtled through the air.

Tex ducked even as he fired. The knife struck the woodwork of the window-frame an inch from his head. At almost the same moment Tex fired again and this time didn't miss. Rocky staggered back and then Tex was on him.

As he dealt with him, putting him out for the time being, Buck Forbes was on Jeb. He straightened with a gun in his hand. Tex grabbed Rocky's and thrust it at Linda.

'OK, after me, you last, Forbes,' he snapped. 'Don't ask questions, they'll keep.'

Just for a moment his hand gripped Linda's bare arm. Then he was making for the door. Jeb, like Rocky, was now out, having been clubbed by Buck.

There was pandemonium now in the hotel. Shots were being fired, men were shouting and from somewhere there came a woman's scream.

Tex led the way out of the room. A guy came at him. There was no room to use a gun. Tex sidestepped and then his left hook took the guy on the chin, putting him out. He slumped to the floor and the party went on. The passage leading past the poker room and then the Parson's office, was deserted for the time being; but then, out of the

Parson's office came a man . . . it was Sam Steel, gun in hand. As he came he fired, back into the room.

Tex came level with him, was recognized. Through the open door of the room he saw two other guys, recognized them both. One was the guy he knew was called Snake, the other was Doc Black. The desk was lying on its side, papers scattered on the floor from drawers half-open.

Snake had a knife in his hand. Sam's shot had evidently missed, for neither Snake nor the Doc were wounded. Snake's hand came up with the knife but before he could throw it Tex had fired from the hip. Snake fell back. Another shot cracked out. Buck Forbes had fired, but not at the Doc or Snake. The Parson himself had rounded an angle in the passage. He ducked back, unhurt.

What Sam was doing here Tex didn't know, nor was this exactly the moment to talk about it. Nor was it known what the Kid and the others were doing, but from the saloon came the uproar of fighting and shots were still being fired. Tex grabbed Linda, thrust her across the room towards the window giving on to the alley. Snake was out. The Doc had crumpled under a blow from the butt of Sam's gun and for the moment was also out of action.

Tex thrust up the window. Linda didn't need to be told what to do. She swung lightly over the still and came to the ground outside in the alley.

After that it was simple enough. Main Street was deserted, all the uproar coming from inside the hotel itself. What loungers had been in the street had been attracted into the building. Within a few minutes of making the getaway from the office the party, now four in number, were riding away, with no pursuit. They'd grabbed ponies from the tethering rail and nobody had even seen them doing it. They left the hotel still in the grip of confusion and wild fighting.

Within the hour they'd reached the hideout the Kid had described, reached it without incident, a boulder-strewn declivity amongst the foothills. And when they reached it they found the Kid, Bluebell and Slick waiting for them. Tex hadn't known the way, had been forced to scout around to pick up the right trail. The night was dark, with no moon showing. The Kid and his party had bypassed them and arrived first.

There was somebody else with them – Werner of the Block Diamond, menaced by the gigantic Bluebell, whose gun was pressed into the guy's ribs.

They'd picked up Werner on the way, it seemed. He'd been snooping around amongst the hills.

'Sure, we brought him along,' said the Kid. 'I guess I got somethin' to tell you, Scarron. Look after Werner, Bluebell.'

'Ah sure will, Kid,' was the grim reply, 'He won't get away from me 'cept dead.'

The Kid had plenty to tell Tex. He and his buddies had created a diversion all right, and had got away. Just how he didn't explain, nor did it matter. They'd got away.

'I got somethin' here,' added the Kid, thrusting his hand into his pocket and producing a paper. 'It was in the Parson's pocket . . . I guess I didn't bump the guy off, some of his boys interrupted, but I slugged him . . . that was after you'd scrammed. But I got this paper. It explains a whole lot.'

It did . . . and that wasn't the only explanation made. Linda was with Buck over the other side of the declivity; Tex, the Kid, Slick and Sam were on their own.

Briefly Sam explained that for the past twenty-four hours he'd been hiding up waiting for nightfall. He and Pop had split up when they'd gone scouting after Tex had left the first hideout. Sam had got back in time to witness the end of the Parson's attack and see the prisoners being taken away. It had been impossible to do anything. Sam had gone under cover, had spent the day working out what to do. In the end, when Pop hadn't shown up, he'd gone down to the River and had broken into the hotel.

'I guess it was a fool thing to do,' he added, 'but I heard a couple o' the Parson's boys talkin' an' they let out between 'em you were in the lock-up. I thought maybe I could get you out . . . it don't signify, you made it without me.'

Tex nodded. Sure, they'd made it, with Bluebell's help, but that didn't mean he didn't appreciate Sam's courage. It had needed some to take on the bunch single-handed.

'I got rumbled,' continued Sam, 'but that don't matter now . . . I saw Pop. He was with the Parson in the office, talkin' all friendly, an' there was money passin', wads o' dollars. They didn't see me, I was peekin' through the side window, that was 'fore I got rumbled.' He paused, while Tex, grasping the implications of this, stared. 'That ain't all, Tex . . . the guy Brady is dead meat. I found him in the poker room, knifed in the back. I guess maybe he knew too much.'

Tex stood there with the paper the Kid had given him. That paper proved that Werner had been blackmailed, but it didn't seem important right now. Pop Dwight . . . friendly with the Parson, leaving the hideout before the attack, disappearing, joining up with the Parson and taking a whole lot of dough from him. It all added up. Maybe Brady had carried word to the Parson about the hideout, but who had given him the tip? Now Tex came to think about it there hadn't been a lot of chance of Brady getting close enough to the hideout to be sure of his facts, not with Slick on guard; but he hadn't needed to, not if he'd been slipped the word by somebody who did know.

Pop Dwight . . . the Parson's partner. Sure, it all added up, everything. And maybe Dave Brand had got on to him and Pop had put him out . . . there had been time on the night of the murder, there was only Pop's word for what he'd been doing before meeting up with Tex again.

Sure, it all added up. . . .

CHAPTER 17

'I guess I ought to go see Linda's OK. I wouldn't put it past that guy Werner to pull a fast one.'

Buck Forbes sounded mighty worried, would have made for the ruined, decayed shack that stood on the lip of the declivity nearby if Tex hadn't stopped him.

'She's OK, Buck. There's Slick there with his trigger finger itchin', an' there's Bluebell. Werner won't try nothin', he's safe enough. I want to talk to you. Linda's all right in the shack.'

More than two hours had elapsed since the rendezvous at the new hideout had been kept. The party was still lying up; and by now Tex knew a whole lot, had done some thinking and was now ready to talk about the set-up as it had been revealed by what Sam had reported.

The Kid had sure pulled a fast one in stationing Bluebell at the River in Graw's shop. Tex knew now that it had been Bluebell, eaves-dropping, which she was might good at in spite of her bulk, who had tipped off Linda about the scheme to frame Tex for the murder; who had thus discovered that Tex was on the level, against the Parson.

Tex knew now that Pop was the guy behind the rackets, working with the Parson. It was evident how he'd bluffed all along the line. He'd been arrested at the Bar X, had allowed himself to be; but he'd have worked it that he was cleared of complicity in the killing of Dave Brand. The arrest had been more bluff.

Bluebell was the Kid's buddy. The Kid hadn't let on about her except to Linda because he was being careful with Tex and the others, new recruits. He was a careful guy in some ways – and smart. Tex knew now that down at the hotel he'd managed to lay hands on some of the Parson's dollars, to repay himself for all his trouble, Bluebell helping him, no doubt. That was OK by Tex, who had to use the tools that were at hand. The Kid was one of them. Bluebell and the Kid had come in handy. Right now Bluebell was with Slick in the shack. Buck was anxious about Linda but she'd be OK.

She'd been grabbed by Jeb while roaming the hills searching for Sam after she heard about the affair at the first hideout. Nothing had happened to her, but quite a lot would have happened after the Parson had attended to his other prisoners – or so Tex reckoned from what Linda and Buck had told him.

Buck's anxiety didn't make Tex feel any happier. He reckoned he was odd man out in this particular set-up. It was his own fault for falling for a girl. He pushed aside all thought of the girl. Buck, Sam and the Kid were waiting for him to talk.

'We can forget Werner,' he said. 'We know now for sure the Parson was blackmailin' him, but it don't matter 'cept we've got to keep him close an' not let him get down to the River to take word to the Parson we're up here.' He paused and then added, 'I reckon you guys are satisfied that Pop Dwight is the guy behind the Parson an' took us for a ride?'

Sam Steel nodded.

'Sure, Tex, there ain't no other way o' workin' it out. He acted mighty smart.'

Tex stuck his hands in his gun-belt. His face was grim.

'That's right. He was after me that first night but when I held him up he bluffed fast. You can easy work out how he acted after that. He knew what we were plannin'. I reckon he warned the Parson I was goin' down to the hotel, but he didn't know I was goin' to start a fire an' that took the Parson by surprise. He left the hotel but he came back rememberin' what Pop had said. Only I got him, so he bluffed. Then there's Dave's murder. . . .'

Tex continued, outlining his theory regarding the killing. According to that theory Pop had killed Dave, probably because Dave had found him out, knew who he was. This idea provided a motive, about the only one Tex could work out. He judged, too, that Pop had intended to follow to the hotel to make sure of Tex but then the Dave angle broke and he had to look after the guy who knew too much. He could have got on to the fact that Dave did know too much via Brady. And later he killed Brady, at the hotel, because he could be dangerous.

'That's provided he knew who Pop was,' added Tex. 'He told us 'bout Brady in the first place, but I reckon that was bluff. He had to make sure we didn't start in suspectin' him . . . we knew by then that the Parson had got on to a whole lot he couldn't have known unless some guy had told him. So Pop brought in Brady makin' out he maybe had overheard us talkin'. Sure, some o' this is guessin' but I reckon it was somethin' like that.'

It looked that way. There couldn't be much doubt in view of what Sam had reported, that Pop was the guy behind the Parson. Most factors worked in with this. Pop could have met up with Brady for example in the hills near the first hideout – or maybe another of the bunch – and sent word to the Parson. There had been time. And Pop hadn't showed up again, had kept out of the way.

Everything added up, pretty well every move taken fitted into the belief that Pop Dwight, seeming such a nice guy, had foxed and bluffed and been behind the set-up all the time.

The movements of Doc Black and Poston on the night of the murder could have meant nothing except they were scouting around Bar X territory on the look-out for Tex. Or maybe they'd helped Pop in the killing, though this wasn't likely. Tex reckoned that nobody but the Parson knew who Pop was. And he had a hunch that Pop himself had killed Dave, for the motive already explained.

Buck's movements on the night of the killing had now been revealed. He'd been out after some lost steers. Tex took his word for this. Buck had changed sides having at last rumbled the Parson.

As though reading Tex's thoughts, Buck spoke up now.

'I been a fool,' he said bitterly, 'lettin' the Parson take me for a ride. He's after the Lazy Y.' He turned to Tex and added, 'I got a lot to be grateful to you for. I'm sorry 'bout the lynchin'. I'd got you all wrong.'

'That's OK, Buck, forget it.'

The Kid broke in. He reckoned, he said, that it was time they started working out what move to take next. They knew Pop Dwight was their man, but how to get him? There had been enough time wasted up here already.

'Sure, that's right,' agreed Sam. 'What we goin' to do, Tex? You ain't bankin' on spendin' the rest o' your natural up here?'

'We can get Pop,' he said, 'an' it won't give us too much trouble, I guess.'

Buck peered at him through the darkness.

'You reckon not?' And then, 'I guess Linda ain't takin' this so well? She was mighty fond o' Pop Dwight.'

Buck was right. Linda had been indignant when Tex had talked to her. The idea that Pop was a crook, was behind the Parson, setting up the rackets at Grant's River, not only appalled her but she refused to believe it. For a bit Tex had found it pretty difficult, but eventually she let him talk. By the time he'd finished she'd come round to his opinion – she'd had to.

'She took it hard,' agreed Tex, 'but that ain't the point right now. I guess we got to do some talkin' 'bout the future, not the past. You ain't lettin' up, Sam? You want the guy even though it is Pop?'

Sam spat eloquently. Sure he wanted the guy, whoever he was.

'OK, then I guess . . .'

Tex got no farther for away to the west came the crack and flash of a six-shooter. It was followed by another shot and another. The bullets fell short, did no damage, but the next volley might not be so harmless. The four men flung themselves down, finding plenty of cover behind scattered boulders. The Kid brought up his gun and as another shot cracked out, fired back, aiming at the flash.

The next moment pretty near a dozen guns spoke from the western flank, and this time the range was shorter, for the lead came too close for comfort. Whoever was firing was coming closer . . . it didn't take much working out who the enemy was.

'Heck, the Parson's on to us again,' muttered Sam, and fired back at the flashes swiftly.

As he did so a fresh attack was launched from the east, catching the four between two fires. They had cover from the west but not from the east.

It was evident that in the darkness the hideout had been pretty well surrounded. Evident, too, and not needing any other evidence, that Sam was right – the Parson had caught up with them again.

Tex took charge, the Kid not arguing on that score.

'Buck, Kid, get to the shack,' ordered Tex. 'Sam, you come with me. . . .'

He was obeyed pronto. The darkness hadn't played in for them up to now, allowing the hideout to be approached, but now it worked for them. The Kid and Buck slid away towards the ruined shack which had once been inhabited by a squatter long since dead. The Kid knew what he was doing, didn't use his gun and stopped Buck using his. He wasn't giving away the fact that they were beating it.

Tex moved as well, with Sam, but east, not towards the shack. He reckoned that the first attack had been a feint to draw their attention; that meant that the main attack was being launched from the east. It was that way Tex went.

Sam moved silently alongside Tex. By now the Kid and Buck must have reached the shack. The hideout was dead quiet. Tex reckoned that the Parson must be mighty worried what with one thing and another and had got up here as quick as he could move when he got word that the guys he wanted so badly were still hanging around.

The enemy were still firing, and coming on towards the hideout from both sides. Tex and Sam could pin-point their positions by the flashes from the six-shooters. They slid away into the darkness, turned north, passed round the end of the advancing contingent from the west and so came to the rear of the bunch.

'You ain't aimin' to slip 'em?' asked Sam. 'What 'bout Linda? If she's in the shack. . . .'

He got no farther for a shot rang out close at hand and the bullet spurted dust a couple of inches in front of Sam. The two flung themselves down. Evidently some of the Parson's bunch had been coming on behind the main party and had sighted Tex and Sam. Tex's gun spoke swiftly and was answered by a cry. Against the skyline Tex saw a figure perk into view, fling up arms wildly and fall back.

And then there was a cry behind him. He swung round, and at that moment the moon came out from behind the clouds for the first time that night. Tex saw the Parson clearly, crouched on the top of an outcrop, gun levelled at him . . . and even as he fired a figure pounched from behind, grabbed the Parson. The bullet didn't miss, but it didn't kill, due to the intervention of Bluebell, as Tex could now see. As he and Sam made a move the struggling figures at the top of the out-crop lost their hold and sagged down the steep side. There was a wild confusion of arms and legs and then they'd reached the bottom, the Parson underneath. Bluebell, bandanna come adrift, yellow dress torn and dirty, sat astride the Parson, her face split in a huge, malicious grin. As Tex came up she raised her gun and crashed the butt across the Parson's head. He was out – for a long time.

Another figure materialized and yet another behind him. The Kid and Slick came up . . . they'd evidently left the shack and moved around behind the eastern bunch. Bluebell had been in time to put paid to the Parson.

'Ah guess he won't be givin' any more trouble for a bit,' she grinned. And then, to Tex, 'You caught it, then, honey . . . too bad, ah reckoned ah'd got him in time.'

Tex was in pain, the bullet having hit him in the left shoulder.

'I'm OK.'

And then, overlaying the firing still proceeding from the direction of the hideout, came noise of another sort. Mounted men were approaching, a heck of a lot of them judging by the thunder of hoofs. Almost at once more shooting broke out, but not from near the hideout.

Tex swung round . . . the moonlight, now strong, revealed riders sweeping down on the hideout from three directions, from west and north and east. The guys were firing as they came.

Sam let fall an oath. As far as he could judge there were pretty near fifty guys coming on, all mounted, bringing their ponies swiftly and skilfully along narrow goat tracks, some straight over the rough ground.

'We got to get,' he rasped, 'the Parson must've brought up every guy he's got . . .'

He broke off, for dead ahead of him the first of the riders from the east came plainly into view. It was Pop Dwight.

Sam's Colt came up, but then Tex moved. Disregarding the pain from his wounded shoulder, the blood now seeping down over the stuff of his shirt, his hand came out, grabbed Sam's gun, jerked it up. The shot cracked but the bullet spent itself harmlessly in the air. Then Sam was down, skilfully thrown, and Tex was standing over him with his gun menacing him.

'OK, Steel, you've reached the end,' he rasped. 'These guys are Governor's rangers . . . an' Pop brought 'em here. You've been mighty clever foxin', Steel, bluffin' me, workin' it so that it looked

Pop was the guy we were after, but you ain't the only one to fox. I've been foxin' ever since we got here, keepin' you happy. When the Parson comes round he'll talk . . . this is the end for you. You made a mighty bad mistake that put me on to you, Steel.'

Sam Steel lay on the ground staring up at Tex. But now his face had changed, was a vindictive mask of hate. He made a sudden swift move, got to his feet, but as he did so the Kid was on him. There was a cry of pain and Sam was down again, lying there twisted, expertly thrown. He lay huddled, whimpering with pain from a broken arm.

'That'll square my account with you,' said the Kid, disregarding the wild confusion all around him as Governor York's rangers swept down amongst the Parson's boys, now disorganized and outnumbered.

Pop Dwight came up, swung from the saddle. Tex grabbed his arm.

'Linda, is she OK, Pop?'

'Sure, she got to us in time. She's comin' along any minute. York had a couple o' rangers ride with her.'

Tex's hand came out as half a dozen mounted men rode up and dismounted.

'Thanks, Pop,' he said. 'It's worked out OK.'

The Parson and Sam Steel were being looked after by the rangers. The noise of fighting was fading into the distance as the Parson's boys broke off the unequal battle and fled. Then Buck came racing up on foot.

'Say, Tex, the Kid an' Slick an' the black are clearin', I guess. . . .'

Tex nodded.

'Sure, that was the arrangement. They don't want to talk to the Governor,' And then, as Buck stared bewildered at Sam Steel, being brought to his feet, still whimpering with pain, obviously under arrest, he added, 'It's OK, Buck, Steel's our guy, the guy behind the Parson.'

Buck Forbes switched baffled eyes from Sam to Pop Dwight.

'I don't get it,' he muttered. 'This guy . . .'

'This guy is all right,' was Tex's reply. 'I'll give you the dope later.'

*

He did give the dope, much later, when the next day those significantly connected with the affair congregated in the sheriff's office down at the River. By then there had been a clean-up. The Parson and most of his boys, those that didn't get away, were under arrest. So were Poston, one-time sheriff but that no longer, Snake, Jeb and Doc Black, who'd worked in with the Parson. The River was occupied by York's rangers, sixty of them, recruited by the new Governor to clean up Arizona.

In the sheriff's office were crowded York himself, Tex, Pop Dwight, Buck Forbes, a couple of York's rangers and Linda Forbes, looking as fresh as though she'd not undergone the experiences that had been hers. Tex reckoned she was looking lovely.

Tex had the floor, on the invitation of York, a stubby, middle-aged man shrewd of eye – and as had been proved, swift in action. Tex was doing the talking.

For York's benefit he'd explained the sequence of events up to the arrival at the new hideout. Some of it York already knew from Pop Dwight, but not all. Now he did.

'I reckoned Pop was our guy,' said Tex, 'after Sam had told his story. But then I suddenly got wise. I don't know why I thought of it just then, I ought to have picked it up a long time before . . . but I didn't. I got it sudden when I was workin' out how Pop could have killed Dave. Sam made a bad slip. He said he'd only just found Dave when Pop and me turned up, five minutes before, he said. But that wasn't possible if Linda was tellin' the truth – an' I reckoned she was. Sure, she was tellin' the truth, so Sam was lyin'. Linda saw him with Dave a long time before. After that she had time to ride around, meet up with me, talk and then there was time for Pop an' me to get back to the Bar X. Sam couldn't have made a mistake, not of half an hour at least. He was lyin', and that made me think. After that I talked to Linda, alone, an' she told me Pop had gone for you, Governor. He couldn't have been near the hotel when Sam said he saw him, he was with you twenty miles away.'

From Linda, Tex learned that on the previous night, after the attack on the first hideout, she'd met Pop. He'd heard that York was twenty miles away after some rustlers. He agreed with Linda to ride for the Governor and put him wise to what was going on at the River. After that Linda was grabbed.

'It made it sure Sam was the guy we wanted,' continued Tex. 'Work it out an' you'll find all the reasons why Pop could have been the Parson's partner applied to Sam. The Parson's talked now an' we know Sam put out Dave because he'd rumbled him. Otherwise he'd have followed me to the hotel. He had to make out he was away from the house when Dave was killed so he lied about when he found him, not knowin' that Linda had seen him. When he found that out I guess he was mighty worried, but he banked on me not realisin' that the two tales didn't link up.'

Pop Dwight puckered his forehead. What about the letter Sam had written to Tex asking him to come to the River?

'Sure, that foxed me at first. But it's easy enough. He knew Dave had written so he wrote himself by way of bluff. He knew I'd come for Dave . . . he aimed to fox me from the beginnin' makin' out he wanted me, too. He aimed to get me when I did show up.'

Pretty well everything was known now, both the Parson and Sam having talked. Sam hadn't told the Parson he was after Tex, not until after he'd arrived at the settlement. He'd mentioned him but only casually. He aimed to work it so he was cleared of any complicity in the Brand murder, but let himself be arrested by way of continuing his bluff in case anything went wrong. The Parson had hoped to get Sam. He'd had word via Brady, who had been tipped off by Sam, that Tex and the rest were at the first hideout. He'd planned to get up there quick enough to get Sam as well, bump him off, but Sam had been too quick for him, hadn't returned to the hideout. Then the Parson had arranged with Snake to do the job, reckoning that Sam was bound to show up at the hotel.

He had shown up and Snake would have laid for him but then the prisoners escaped and there was no chance. Sam killed Brady because the guy knew who he was, always had known. It had been useful having him up at the Bar X, but in the end it had been necessary to kill him before he talked. Sam had gone on bluffing, had escaped with Tex and the rest to the new hideout. Not all this had been revealed, but from the Parson's tale and Sam's, taken independently, it could all be worked out. Sam hadn't known the Parson was after him. He'd still been aiming to get Tex at the new hideout, but Tex was on to him by then and watched him, giving him no chance.

Tex had bluffed for a change. Linda had been appalled when Tex started to talk to her in the shack, making it look at first he thought Pop was guilty. Then she told her tale and agreed to do what Tex wanted. He sent her to make contact with York and Pop, banking on the fact that by then they'd be on their way to the River, using the only trail open to them via Indian Creek. She was to bring them to the hideout.

'Sure, she wasn't in the shack, I was kiddin',' said Tex, 'I had to. Werner wasn't there, either. He played in an' went down to the River to tip off the Parson where we were. It all worked out OK.'

Tex knew that Sam was his man but he couldn't prove it. He reckoned if he could tempt the Parson to bring his boys to the hideout and trap him when York showed up, he could work the proof. The Parson would talk, he had no doubt. The only way he could get the Parson was to bring him to the hideout. Werner had done that for him. When he had finished York spoke up. The plan had worked but Tex had taken a risk – a double risk. York's rangers might not have been contacted in time, and anyway Tex might not have been able to hold the Parson's bunch until they arrived.

'Sure, I know, but I was willin' to take the chance. I wanted the guy who killed Dave.'

The Governor grunted. There were two other points. What had happened to the Kid and his buddies? How had Tex persuaded Werner to play in with him?

Tex shrugged his shoulders.

'I reckon the Kid's mighty smart,' he drawled. 'He vamoosed quick. I couldn't stop him. I reckon maybe I'm glad at that,' he added, 'he did me a good turn an' you, Governor, come to that. We wouldn't have broken this racket without him. I let him in on the bluff.'

The Governor permitted himself a thin smile. He could see through a brick wall as well as the next man.

'And Werner?'

'Werner's a good guy,' was the reply. 'He wasn't doin' anythin' when the Kid got him, only ridin' around. He agreed to play in an' take word to the Parson, that's all.'

The Governor accepted it, or seemed to. But later still, when Linda Forbes talked to Tex, she brought up the subject again. She and Tex were alone in the office.

'The Kid told me about the paper he took off the Parson,' she said. 'Seems it proved Werner was bein' blackmailed.'

He nodded. He wasn't keeping anything back from her.

'Sure . . . Werner played in an' I promised he'd have that paper back. Seems he slipped up ten years ago, took part in a hold-up an' the Parson got to know, got proof. Werner's OK now, I gave him the paper. He's been goin' straight for ten years he says an' I guess that's the truth. We got somethin' to thank him for.'

'Yes . . . and I've got a lot to thank you for, Tex. If it hadn't been for you, Tex. . . .'

He brushed aside her thanks.

'It's OK . . . now I guess you can get on with marryin' Buck. I wish you plenty o' happiness.'

He turned away but then swung back as she spoke.

'Marry Buck? What put that idea into your head? I'm aimin' to marry a sheriff,' she added.

He stared at her, down at her, for he towered above her. His wounded shoulder was now healing nicely.

'I don't get it. I thought you an' Buck . . . what's this 'bout a sheriff?'

She was flushed, her eyes were bright.

'You glad I don't want to marry Buck?'

He took a step forward, gripped her arm.

'What's the game? You know darn well I . . . you know what I feel 'bout you, I guess. You're a woman, ain't you?'

She smiled up at him.

'Yes, I'm a woman. I know, Tex . . . I told you, I aim to marry a sheriff.' Then, as a variety of emotions, including bafflement, followed each other across Tex's face, 'Hasn't York told you he's lookin' for a new sheriff for the River? I guess you'll accept the job, won't you?'

For a moment he continued to stare down at her. His eyes followed the lovely line of her throat, rising from the neck of her open shirt, followed it up to the fine bones of the face under the velvet skin . . . to the blue eyes, the dark hair. And then he spoke, just one word.

'Heck. . . .'

After that he had something else to do besides talk. He found it more enjoyable, too. Come to that, so did Linda.

Things had worked out all right.